THE LEGENDS OF MERLIN

AND

THE MYTHICAL SWORDS

DOUG MCPHILLIPS

Also, by Doug McPhillips:

Other Visionary Stories:

NOVELS.
From Darkness to Light.
Awakened to my Gutted Dream.
The Sword of Discernment.
Santiago Traveller.
I Prophet.
Master's at my table.
The Guru of Jerusalem.
We are upside down. (Biography)
The Wicklow Way.
The Adventures of Ace McDice.
Instant Karma & Grace.
The Credo.
Reflections of an Old Man.
Reincarnation of the Assassin
Masters of Introspection.
Journey to a hermit's haven.
The Rise and Rise of a 4th Reich
Grandad's tales are tall and true.
Into Action: Alcoholics for Jesus
Lightbulb Moments
For Pete's sake
Walking in My Shadow
A Pilgrim's Last Hurrah
A Camino Guide Book

Country Camino. (Album).
Santiago Traveller. (Album).
Soul Fact. (Album).

Doug McPhillips, Circa 2025. ISBN 978-1-763804-0-9

National Library of Australia Catalogue-in-Publication data: New Holy Bible, International Version, Hodder & Stoughton, 1980. Daily Reflections, 11th Print, AA World Service 2014.
Journey to the Inner Mountain, Hodder & Staughton, 2002.
The Choice is always ours, Jove Publishing, 1997.
The Sword of Discernment, Ingram Spark. Doug McPhillips 2014
Santiago traveller, Ingram Spark, Doug McPhillips, 2018.
Lightbulb Moments, Ingram Spark, Doug McPhillips, 2025
The Mythical Journey Simon & Schuster, 1999
Stories of King Arthur and the Knights of the Round Table
Rupert S. Holland, Amazon Books, 2023
King Arthur and his Knights Howard Peel British Press 1911
Legends of King Arthur and his Knights, Malory and Knowles, 2020
Notebook Research 2025.
Google research- Authors Unknown.

DEDICATION

For those who are open to the mystical,
the fantasy, and spiritual consciousness.
This story is for you.

- Doug McPhillips (Merlin's scribe)

Content.

To bring forth.

As I sit in the shadows of my thoughts, the flickering light dances upon the stone walls, a serpent of memories winding through my mind. I am Merlin, once a wild Celtic prophet, torn between realms and destinies, destined to play many roles in the grand tapestry of fate.

My life began under the tumultuous skies of ancient Britain, born of an earthly mother and a father from another world. They aimed to turn me into an instrument of darkness—an antichrist—but divine intelligence stepped in, changing my course. I emerged not as a villain but as a protector of good, entwining my fate with that of a king yet to come. My life began under the stormy skies of ancient Britain, born to an earthy mother of earth and a demon avatar from another world.

Ah, Arthur! The boy who would become a symbol of nobility! I mentored him, guiding him to pull the sword from the stone, a testament to his birthright and the heavy crown of leadership he was destined to wear. I watched as Camelot rose, a beacon of hope and wisdom—my efforts woven into its very foundation. Alas, it, too, would falter and fall, as all kingdoms of the earthly realm have done since, and will continue to do. Yet, my past haunted me, whispers of my half-demon heritage casting long shadows over my heart. No longer tormented by what I was, I became a servant of destiny, embracing my role as a wise advisor to kings, saints and spiritual seekers alike, where I blended magic with morality. Symbols became my language, my way of seeing beyond the veil of time. I witnessed reminders of my purpose flicker and fade like distant stars. It is said I beheld the archangel Gabriel wielding his flaming sword, casting Lucifer and his minions from the heavens. I marvelled at the celestial clash, a reminder of the eternal struggle between light and darkness. I later aided St. James, appearing in the sky as a harbinger of hope, guiding Christians against the Moors in battle with an ethereal sword in hand. My life was filled with intertwined myths, a dance of truth and legend. I bestowed the magical sword on Charlemagne, a gift meant to inspire courage, which would echo through time. I watched as Roland fell in Roncesvalles Pass, his sacrifice a testament to the weight of destiny and the tumultuous fate of heroes.

Yet, in my later years, I became a tragic figure, consumed by loneliness and a touch of madness. The vast expanse of knowledge weighed heavily on my soul, a lonely genius burdened with wisdom. I found myself ensnared by the enchanting Lady of the Lake—a captivating force that led me to my ultimate downfall. Captivity in a cave became my fate, trapped by my affection for her. I realised then that no matter how powerful someone may be, love can turn even the strongest into the frailest of mortals. And so, I sit, reflecting on my journey from the wild depths of prophecy to the ethereal heights of magic, a bridge between the moral and the eternal. In time, my story will be told—the legend of Merlin, the wise old man, who shaped kingdoms, wielded secrets, and ultimately learned that even the greatest wizards must face their destinies.

My tale unfolds through the ages, embodying the eternal struggle between wisdom and folly, light and dark, and the unfulfilled longing for connection in a world rife with magic and mystery. The legend of my life is told here by the guiding hand of the writer of this, my life's journey from prophecy to magic, to wonder and mystery, to that of the aging swords of Durandal, Excalibur, and Gram, at the dawn of divine light, heroism, loyalty, royal authority, and courage. This story is for this generation and those who will come after. It is a never-ending journey, as you will soon discover.

Merlin

Myths, Legends and Folklore.

In the broader tapestry of Merlin's medieval legends, another tale took root—one of the confident Apostle James, who, according to Christian tradition, reached the Iberian Peninsula in A.D. 40. A few years after the death and resurrection of his Master, Jesus, James carried the same message the Twelve had first received: "Repent, believe, for the kingdom of heaven is at hand." He taught that love of neighbour must eclipse love of self and that true disciples would "do unto others as they would have others do unto them." Christ had charged these rough-hewn fishermen to become fishers of souls, and James obeyed.

Travelling by boat, he set foot on Spain's rocky shores and preached among Celtic tribes steeped in polytheism, ancestor reverence, and nature worship. A man of action more than eloquence, James embodied his Gospel through deeds, trusting that example spoke louder than words. Yet after four years, he had won only seven converts. One evening, seated on a boulder near the fishing village of Finisterre—then thought to be the world's edge—he despaired of completing his mission.

That night, the Virgin Mary, still living in Bethany, appeared to him in a dream. She urged him to build a church in her honour on a stark granite outcrop at Muxía, where fishermen cast their nets into the Atlantic. James obeyed, raised the shrine, and soon returned to Jerusalem. There he preached another four years before King Herod ordered his beheading in A.D. 44, making him the first apostolic martyr. So it came to pass that the Apostles sent James' body with his head by barge adrift toward Spain, Viking style, where it was met by his seven followers, near Iria Flavia, present day Padron, who took his remains to a nearby hill and buried them.

Thereupon, he was forgotten for nearly eight hundred years until 813 AD.

It is written that a Christian hermit, around this time, named Pelayo, saw, on Mount Liberedon, a shining light [probably the Milky Way] which led him to James' grave and the remains of two of his disciples, Atarasio and Teodoro. The local bishop authenticated the remains, and to honour the saint, King Alfonso 111 built a chapel, which drew a modest number of pilgrims. So, the Cathedral de Santiago was built in his honour, and upon completion in 1120, the remains were encased in a tomb below the altar. Pilgrims have flocked there since medieval times to pay homage and, in some cases, to seek indulgences.

The Camino de Santiago might seem like a purely Christian journey, but many people of other faiths, or none at all, walk The Way of St. James, just as thousands did in medieval times. A legend about the humble shrine of St James tells of the battle of Clavigo, between Islamic Muslim invaders and Spanish Christian soldiers. The final battle was about to be had, but snow and rain resulted in a truce until winter's end. On the Iberian Peninsula, the remains of St. James were discovered at the time. The area was rich in silver, gold and bronze, and was eagerly sought and fought over.

When Pelayo discovered the bones and some fossil remains, the local bishop promptly declared them to be those of St. James, blessed them, and celebrated a Mass in honour of the find. A myth thus spread during the Battle of Clavijo that followed stated that St. James appeared mounted on a white steed, holding a fiery sword aloft, leading the Spanish into battle. The image of St. James became a convenient rallying point for Christian support at the frontier of the Muslim-Christian struggle, bolstering financial backing for Christian dominance in Iberia.

It has been foretold that Christian soldiers spread some of St. James' ashes over the battlefield before the final charge, while the Muslims, not to be outdone, held a mummified arm of the Prophet Muhammad as a guiding symbol. Although the legend persists that James appeared on the battlefield of Clavijo, it seems to be a direct result of the Christians regaining the upper hand in Spain, but it is merely a story. There is no record of a battle in historic documents. In fact, St. James, as the best of scholars seem to agree, never came to Spain. There is no earthly reason why his body should have been brought to Galicia, and nothing in the Acts of the Apostles in the Bible mentions his death. James died several centuries before Islam was conceived, probably never mounted a horse in his life, and indeed never killed a Muslim to live up to the name of being the "James, Moor Slayer".

Why, then, should this writer start this story on St. James rather than Merlin? In truth, the writer has walked the Way of St. James three times before, and despite his scepticism about the story's validity, he wants to do so again. The logical, linear brain is overwhelmed by its own imagination. This writer is more inclined to heed the guidance of Merlin than his own sense of belief. Well, think of Merlin not as a single moment in Arthur's lifetime but as a restless current of wonder that surfaces whenever history or man reaches a crossroads.

When Saint James stepped onto Spain's mist-hung coast, that current was already swirling: the same raw peninsula where iron-age druids whispered to oak and star, the same frontier whose skies would one day shimmer with the Milky Way guiding pilgrims to

Compostela. Merlin's lore tells that he could ride such thresholds—places where the mundane thins and the miraculous seeps through.

Merlin was always there in the shadow land. He watches the Apostle wrestle with discouragement at Finisterre, then kindles hope with a midnight vision of the Virgin. He sees James launch a stone boat that defies wind and tide, just as a boy-king once drew a sword that defied iron and law. Two acts, one pattern: heaven bending the rules to mark a chosen path.

Across the centuries runs a single, silvery thread: Saint James lands on Galicia's wind-scoured shore to preach repentance, his stone boat and seaside shrine sowing the first seeds of the Camino; eight hundred years later pilgrims still follow the Milky Way to Compostela, their scallop shells mapping the Way, echoing the "singing" blades—Gram, Durandal, Excalibur—that once chose kings and heroes. Bridging these moments is Merlin, shape-shifter and sage, who drifts west from Camelot to tune iron into destiny, folding the clarion of Gabriel and the battle cry of Michael into every sword's bright chord. Thus history's plain facts, legend's bright colours, and an unseen current of grace interlock: fishermen become fishers of souls, rough steel becomes covenant, and every traveller—whether apostle, knight, or barefoot pilgrim—steps onto a road where the ordinary rings with enchantment and the mundane hums with celestial design. And to this very day, the routes to Santiago—etched by nature, symbolism, and folklore into the back of every pilgrim's scallop shell—tell of the many ways that lead onward, each milestone marked with the guiding shell that points the Way.

Across the weave of myth and memory, Merlin drifts like a living ley-line, slipping backward and forward through time to nudge imagination into history. Whenever he appears, the veil thins: kings feel the weight of prophecy, warriors glimpse a higher chivalry, saints and sinners alike awaken to the tremor of unseen purpose. In his hands, a mere ingot of iron is smelted into a conduit of destiny, its edge tuned to the music of the otherworld. So too the stone boat that bore Saint James—whether fact or fable—becomes a floating reliquary whose wake still draws pilgrims to Compostela, inviting the world-weary to cast off their burdens and realign with the life of the spirit. Steel, stone, shoreline: through Merlin's touch, each commonplace substance crackles with miracle, reminding us that the sacred is never farther away than the next sword thrust skyward, the iconic scallop shell mapping out the Way to Santiago, lifted to the light, the next footfall on a pilgrim's pathway.

Now, at this point, I pause, dear reader, to listen to the words of Merlin himself, for they will shed light on his shape-shifting ability to move through time and his mission.

"You might wonder how I tell stories of events that happened even before I was born. That gift—the ability to read lives from the past—comes from the being who fathered me. If you're doubting, look no further than Geoffrey of Monmouth, the first chronicler of Arthur and his knights, who revealed my other-worldly conception. He described how my mother, a devout nun, was visited by an incubus, a demon in human form. From her claim that I had no human father, all the whispers of the formidable, sometimes shadowy powers I possess arose. But remember what I said at the start of this story: The beings from the Otherworld tried to make me into an instrument of darkness—an antichrist—but divine intervention changed my course towards the light."

So, in distinguishing myth from reality, it is worth considering the Avatar Christ here, as those who believe will attest to his coming to save humanity, and that it is not a myth but supported by biblical texts, ancient scrolls, and non-biblical writings from the Roman Empire as a real living man who made the supreme sacrifice for humanity.

For he was conceived by the Holy Spirit and born of a virgin, Jesus entered history as the living revelation of God, embodying in human flesh the self-giving love he came to unveil. Throughout his ministry, he proclaimed and enacted the nearness of the Kingdom of God—healing the sick, welcoming outsiders, and teaching in parables that justice, mercy, and humble obedience mark life under God's reign. Yet his purpose reached beyond proclamation to atonement and reconciliation. By freely embracing the cross, he bore humanity's sin and estrangement, and in rising on the third day, he shattered the power of death, vindicating his message and opening a new covenant in which all who trust him are reconciled to the Father. Thus, the virgin birth, the Kingdom he announced, and the cross-and-resurrection form one seamless mission: to restore creation by revealing, rescuing, and renewing it through divine love.

And so the ages turned. The Child once cradled in a Bethlehem manger had fulfilled His mission, and the world—now baptised in the hope of resurrection—marched on beneath the same stars that had guided shepherds and sages.

Centuries later, those stars glittered above a different band of travellers: the Frankish host of Carolus Magnus, King Charles—Charlemagne—pressing south across the snow-ribbed passes of the

Pyrenees. Their boots beat the very ridgeway that generations of penitents would one day call the Camino, the Way of Saint James, each milestone already dreaming of the scallop shell. Yet even here, the pulse of older legends could be felt. For in Charlemagne's train rode Roland, whose peerless blade Durandal would flash at Roncesvalles like a cousin to the enchanted swords of earlier lore —Gram of Sigurd, Excalibur of Arthur, the stone-bound brand that Merlin had once foretold would prove a king's right. Thus did history and myth converge upon a single mountain spine: pilgrims walking for absolution, paladins riding for empire, and unseen on the wind the echo of the wizard's prophecy that every righteous sword, whether borne by knight or king, must sooner or later be lifted in the battels that unfolded that left with it the Song of Roland and breathed life again into the imaginations of man evermore.

And so Merlin, guardian of memory and witness of destiny, whispered into the wind: "Come closer, child of dust and dream. Hear the wind as it carries the voices of the fallen. The oak remembers, the stones still speak. For I am Merlin, once the kingmaker, now but the shadow that remembers. For this is the tale of Roland —Paladin of Christendom, son of valour, whose heart was a forge, whose sword was a song, and whose end gave birth to a legend that outlived kings and empires."

So it was that Brittany lay wrapped in mist — a land of druids, wild rivers, and old gods who whispered to stones. There, in the storm-tossed halls of March, a boy was born beneath a night that cracked with thunder. His name was Roland. He grew in the way of wolves and warriors — swift of hand, proud of heart. He was never meant to be ordinary.

Charlemagne, Emperor-to-be, looked upon him and saw what others feared: a spirit unbroken. "Nephew," Charlemagne said the first day he laid eyes upon him, "your arm may yet defend the faith that binds the world." Roland answered, "Then give me the road, uncle, and I will carve the path." And so began the making of a Paladin.

Merlin's whisper: "Crowns do not choose heroes. Storms choose them."

When Charlemagne rose to forge Christendom from chaos,
Roland came forth as a spark from that significant hammer blow
—His sword was quick, his faith unbending, his pride ungoverned.
The emperor saw in him the promise of both victory and tragedy,
And so, he took him under his banner, calling him *nephew* and *son of my spirit.*

Long before the valleys of Spain drank the blood of heroes, before the echo of the Oliphant rolled across the Pyrenees, there was Roland — a boy of Brittany, born of wild winds and restless seas. His land lay on the edge of the Empire, where the faith of Rome met the stubborn freedom of the Celts. Noble of birth, yet greater than lineage was the fire within him —a flame that no obedience could tame, and no danger could quench.

Merlin's whisper: "Here begins the shaping of a hero,
for in fire and blood, a true knight is born."

Brittany, fierce and half-pagan, refused the crown's command. Its druids still whispered to the stones, its chiefs defied the Frankish cross. Roland, Count of the Breton March, led the emperor's captains westward. Through rain and rebellion, he carved his legend, turning back the spears of the Bretons and planting the emperor's banner upon mist-wrapped hills.

Merlin's whisper: "Courage is holy, yet pride shadows the brave. Here, Roland learned both lessons of the Paladin."

To the north rose the Saxons, worshippers of ancient gods. Charlemagne sought to baptise the land in light or blood. Roland rode beside him, steel singing in the forests of the Elbe. For Charlemagne had entrusted the sword of Durangel, which had been imposed on him by angels; it was forged as a singing sword of mystery and magic. In its hilt were a tooth of St. Peter, the blood of St. Basil, a lock of hair of St. Denis, and a fragment of cloth from the Robe of Mary, the mother of Jesus. Roland wielded it at the battle of Eresburg Castle, in the fall of Imminsul, the sacred pagan pillar of the pagans. He wielded victory for the Franks.

He wept — not for the pagans, but for the faith they lost. At Sibig-urb and Paderborn, he faced Widukind, the leader of the Saxon army, whose defiance mirrored his own. With cause and courage, he won the battle.

Merlin's whisper: "A sword of Heaven finds its champion, and destiny takes shape in the hand of the young Paladin."
Roland returned to Brittany and Saxony, Durandal blazing in his hand, a symbol of faith and might. Across Christendom, his deeds spread like wildfire: songs in courts, prayers in monasteries, whispers in villages.

Merlin's whisper: "Fame follows courage, yet the greatest trial waits beyond the mountains."

The year was 778, and Charlemagne had turned his gaze toward Spain. The wind that rolled down from the Pyrenees carried with it a strange omen — a whisper in many tongues, neither Frankish nor

Moorish. In the Emperor's camp, banners snapped against the early summer sky.

For months, emissaries from the emir of Zaragoza had pleaded for aid against their rivals in Córdoba, and Charlemagne, ever the architect of Christendom, saw the chance to extend his reach beyond the mountains. He rode at the head of a glittering host — thousands of Frankish warriors, the Paladins at his side, and at the rear, as guardian of the march, he sent Roland, Count of the Breton March, bearer of Durendal, the sword that no mortal hand would break.

The valley of Roncevaux was narrow and treacherous. Basque warriors, silent as ghosts, descended from the ridges. "Roland!" Oliver cried as the first arrows fell. "Blow the Oliphant! Call the emperor!" Roland raised Durandal high. "No. We shall hold." The battle became a storm. Men fell as if the earth drank them. Roland's horn hung at his side like an unspoken word. Only when the ground was carpeted with the dead — his friends, his brothers — did he lift the Oliphant to his lips. The note that tore from it was no mere sound. It was a cry that shook mountains. His temples burst with the effort. Charlemagne heard, but the hills answered too late. Roland knelt beneath a pine, blood upon his hands, Durandal laid across his knees. "Holy Lord," he whispered, "receive me as I have served." And as the sun fell, so did the last Paladin.

Merlin's Lement

On Christmas Day, in the year of our Lord 800 AD, Pope Leo111 crowned Charlemagne *Emperor of the Romans*. The dream of a Christian empire was realised. Yet in the quiet between the trumpets, Charlemagne's gaze wandered. He remembered a boy with fire in his heart, a warrior beneath a pine, a horn in his hand, a sword of heaven by his side. "If Roland were here," he murmured, he would have laughed at my crown."

It was after Charlemagne was crowned by the Pontiff, Merlin, unseen, walked the corridors of Vatican City, whispered to the streets of stone:

"Empires rise. Kings are crowned.
But the legend of Roland is the truer throne —
carved not of gold, but of memory."

"And so, child of dust and dream, the wind carries his name still. Roland the Paladin, Roland of Durandal, who chose duty over life, courage over comfort, and became the song that no empire can silence. For long after crowns have crumbled, the brave are remembered in the marrow of the world."

In the twilight between dawn and sleep, the old wizard Merlin stood upon the mist-shrouded hill of Logres. His staff was made of yew, and his robe was woven with stars. Around him, the winds carried whispers of centuries yet to come. He lifted his hand, and the mists parted. There, once more, he envisioned the death of Roland, of Durandal, the mighty singing sword, that the Paladin warrior knight had thrust with all his might in his dying breath into a nearby stone face in the valley on the Roncesvalles Pass all those centuries ago.

"Hear me," Merlin intoned, "for what is written may be written again, and the tale of a new vision of a king called Arthur shall not live in one time alone. It shall ride the river of ages, carried by the hands of many tellers."

It came to pass in the 12th Century, when England trembled under the uncertain reign of King Stephen and the land was torn by civil strife, that there lived a quiet cleric and scholar: Geoffrey of Monmouth. A man of letters, yes — but also a man who listened to old whispers carried down through Celtic memory and sacred myth. Among the voices that shaped his pen, none burned brighter than that of Merlin — the wild prophet, the enchanter of tangled bloodlines. For it was told that Merlin was born of a mortal woman, yet his father was not of flesh but of the spirit of where the veil between men and gods thins like mist at dawn.

And one night — whether in waking dream or sacred vision — Merlin's sight opened. He saw beyond the reach of time, and in that vision, he beheld the rise of a king unlike any before him.

"Not by might alone," Merlin whispered to the wind,
 "But by destiny shall he be crowned."

Before him stood a sword embedded in a rock, a blade glowing with the quiet power of the gods. It was not yet named *Excalibur*, but its song echoed with divine promise. As with Roland's fabled Durandal, this sword would not yield to the hands of the strongest knights nor to the cries of the proud. It was a trial set by fate itself.

Then a boy approached — unadorned, unheralded. He put his hand upon the hilt, and the stone shuddered as if remembering an old vow. The sword slid free like a river finding its course. In that moment, destiny took shape: Arthur would be king—a warrior of legend. The seed of Camelot was sown.

Geoffrey, the scholar, felt the tremor of this vision as if it were his own. He took up his quill and began to write what the wild prophet had seen. In "Historia Regum Britanniae", he gave form to a myth born of mist and turned it into the story of a kingdom. His portrait of Arthur was no idle fancy. It was a deliberate act — a hope cast into troubled times. In an age when England was divided, Geoffrey's portrayal of Arthur stood as a unifying figure, a shining ideal of strength, order, and divine right. It was a myth to inspire a king… and perhaps to summon one.

There are many songs sung of Arthur Pendragon, but few burn brighter than the night when he first gained the sword of kings.
In that twilight between myth and faith, when angels and fate still walked the borders of mortal kingdoms, Michael the Archangel, guardian of Heaven's might, was said to have entrusted a blade of divine right to the Lady of the Lake — a keeper of the waters between worlds. The sword gleamed with a light not born of sun or forge, and stars whispered its name before men ever spoke it: Excalibur. "This blade," Michael's voice was said to thunder, "shall not rest in unworthy hands. It shall belong to the king chosen not by ambition, but by destiny."

So the Lady, veiled in mist and power, kept the sword in her silver realm, waiting for the day when a mortal king, blessed by both Heaven and the ancient realm, would claim it. Then Arthur, already crowned by the trial of the sword in the stone, was guided to the lake by Merlin, whose visions stretched far beyond mortal time.
The waters parted as if in reverence, and from their glassy depths

rose a hand of alabaster, holding the sword that would seal his reign.

When Arthur clasped Excalibur, the land itself seemed to breathe for the sword was more than steel. It was royal authority, divine mandate, and the chivalric ideal forged into one.

But the Lady's role did not end with the sword. In another turning of the moon, she found a child orphaned by war — A boy of noble blood, destined for legend. She carried him into her realm beneath the waters, where time flowed differently, where magic and gentle hands shaped him. His name would become Lancelot du Lac — Lancelot of the Lake.
Raised by the Lady and loved by his foster kin, he grew to be the most skilled knight of his age. Where Arthur bore the weight of kingship, Lancelot bore the weight of love — for Guinevere, queen of Camelot, whose beauty and heart bound him in a chain no sword could break.

In the years that followed, when the courts of France bloomed with poetry and pageantry, when troubadours sang of honour and holy quests, there arose a poet — Chrétien de Troyes. He lived beneath vaulted ceilings where crusading knights polished their swords with prayers and ladies of noble birth listened to songs of love that could both exalt and undo a kingdom. He took up the mantle of Geoffrey of Monmouth, whose ink had already carved Arthur's name into the chronicles of kings. But where Geoffrey had written of crowns and destiny, Chrétien spoke of hearts and longing, of knights whose vows were as heavy as their armour.

So through the mists of time, and upon the breath of poets and chroniclers, the kingdom of Camelot rose like a star above the ages. It was a realm of splendour where the Round Table was not merely furniture of oak and gold, but a living symbol of honour, courage, and noble purpose. Here, kings and knights swore fealty not to ambition alone but to a chivalric code—to protect the weak, to uphold justice, and to live as warriors of virtue beneath Arthur's banner.

It was in his telling that the name Lancelot first shone like a star — a knight noble in courage, flawless in chivalry, yet bound to a love forbidden. Guinevere, queen of Arthur's realm, became not merely a consort but the heart of a tragedy. In the hidden chambers of Camelot, between the flickering candles and the songs of court, a love bloomed that no law could sanctify and no sword could silence, for "A knight's heart," Chrétien wrote, "is not of iron, though his blade may be."

For Camelot, built upon oaths of loyalty and virtue, could not endure the storm that followed. As whispers turned to outrage, the Round Table divided: On one side stood Lancelot, shield raised not in rebellion, but in the defence of a love he could not deny. Beside him gathered loyal knights — men who believed in the man as much as the ideal. On the other hand, King Arthur was betrayed not only by his queen's heart but also by the shattering of the sacred code that bound them all, along with another wound of the heart: the betrayal of his favoured noble knight, Lancelot. Then came the deeper wound — the betrayal of Mordred, Arthur's illegitimate son, whose ambition and treachery drove the final nail into the coffin of Camelot's golden age.

From the shadows rose Mordred, Arthur's illegitimate son, born of treachery and fated to bear a crown of ruin. When Camelot stood at its most radiant, Mordred struck at its heart. He betrayed his father, seized the throne, and turned brother against brother. The once-honourable Round Table splintered under the weight of blood and sorrow. Knights who once feasted side by side rode to battle against each other.

Battle thundered across Albion's fields, and the shining court that once stood as the beacon of knighthood fell beneath its own weight. "Thus ends," the poet murmured, "the bright dream of the Round Table. Not with rust upon the sword, but with sorrow in the heart." Yet Chrétien's words, sung in courts far from Camelot, did not mourn as the chronicler does. He romanticised the fall, as poets do: He saw in Lancelot's tragedy the fragility of mortal honour. In Guinevere's love, the perilous power of the heart. In Arthur's ruin, the price of dreaming too high. And so the story spread like fire among noble courts. Knights rode out seeking their own Grail, poets sang of love and valour, and kings learned that no sword — not even Excalibur — could rule the human heart.

On the final battlefield of Camlann, as the mists rolled in and the ravens wheeled overhead, Arthur and Mordred met in a death struggle, father and son bound by prophecy. Excalibur, once the shining emblem of a golden age, was now bathed in the blood of its king. Camelot's towers crumbled not from stone, but from broken vows and shattered hearts.

Through the shrouded mists of the Vale of Camlann, where the clangour of steel gave way to the silence of death, the fate of Arthur Pendragon and his realm was sealed. The once-bright banner of Camelot, gold upon crimson, was torn and bloodied. The earth drank deeply of the sorrow of knights, for on that field lay not only men but the dream of a golden age.

Arthur, grievously wounded by the spear of Mordred, sat slumped upon the battlefield beneath a darkening sky. In his last-ditch effort to save the memory of a once glorious Kingdom now in ruin, he plunged his sword Excalibur into Mordred's heart and in his dying breath, Arthur touched his dead son's head and forgave him for his treachery. Around Arthur, the last of his loyal knights lay fallen, and only Sir Bedivere, steadfast and true, remained at his side. In his fading breath, Arthur spoke not as a king of this world, but as one who now belonged to legend and destiny.

"Take my sword, Excalibur," said the dying king, his voice carrying like a wind through the reeds, "and return it to the Lady of the Lake, from whence it came. For it is not meant to rust in mortal hands."

Three times Sir Bedivere carried the sword to the water's edge, and twice he faltered, struck by the beauty of its jewel-encrusted hilt. To cast it away seemed a crime against the memory of Camelot. But on the third attempt, he flung Excalibur into the misty waters, and the lake answered. From beneath the glassy surface rose a slender arm, pale as moonlight, clothed in white samite. The hand caught the sword by the hilt and raised it high, Excalibur gleaming one last time beneath the fading sun. Then slowly, the arm sank beneath the water, and the sword returned to the Otherworld.

Soon after, a black barge drifted toward the shore, its decks draped in velvet, bearing three queens in mourning veils. They lifted the broken king and laid him upon the bier. The mists thickened, and the barge slipped silently into the waters, bound for Avalon, the Isle of Apples — a place of healing, magic, and eternal sleep.

The bards say Arthur did not die that day. Instead, he passed beyond the mortal realm, awaiting the hour when Britain would need him once more. And thus the sword of kings, gifted by the Archangel Michael and guarded by the Lady of the Lake, was returned to its eternal keeper. Camelot had fallen, yet its spirit endured, carried in the songs of minstrels, in the ink of chroniclers, and in the hearts of generations who yearned for a king who would return.

From Geoffrey of Monmouth's first visions entrusted to him from the mind of Merlin to the romances of Chrétien de Troyes, to the countless poets, monks, and dreamers who followed, the legend of Arthur did not end at Avalon — it became immortal.

In the fading embers of the medieval world, the story begins not in Camelot, but centuries later — in the time of King Edward I of England. Edward, a king of steel and pageantry, prepares for the Eighth Crusade. In his train, he carries not only banners and swords, but a precious manuscript — a collection of Arthurian tales first assembled by Geoffrey of Monmouth for the Earl of Gloucester long ago.

This manuscript, filled with prophecies of Merlin, the rise of Arthur, the sword in the stone, and the Lady of the Lake, has become a royal treasure — a story believed to carry a fragment of divine destiny.

As Edward crosses through Italy, he entrusts the manuscript to Rustichello da Pisa, a gifted storyteller whose words have already stirred noble courts. Rustichello begins to weave these scattered chronicles into *The Romance of King Arthur*, giving Arthur new life in the language of Europe. Through his quill, Arthur's legend spreads like wildfire across France and Italy, growing grander with every telling.

Rustechello de Pisa, once know as the Master of the Arts had woven some unique spell of mystery, and intrigue to his living relic to keep the flame of Arthur King, the Knights of the Round Table and the rise and fall of the kingdom of Camelot a residing relic and template for writers, kings and dreamers to follow, passing through the hands of power and ink, as if Arthur himself had returned to live in glory. For the story takes a turn in the days of Rustechello, who himself is driven by his many talents, to draw upon adventure at the bequest of King Phillip 111 of France a quest to complete three tasks in his employ, to walk as a pilgrim the Camino de Santiago, to report upon the Moor enemies encamped in Spain and draw upon the Sword of Roland embedded in the rock at Roncesvalles Pass and return it to him. For King Philip, this was a test of service and faith. For Rustechello, it became a turning point of myth and destiny.

The Camino's long road etched itself upon his spirit. He walked through misty valleys, past crumbling chapels and the songs of pilgrims, feeling as though the very stones remembered the tread of crusaders and saints. When he reached Roncesvalles, the pass lay wind-scoured and silent, save for the whisper of legend. There, before the pilgrims' shrine, he beheld the stone of Roland, and in it, the hilt of Durandal — the sword once said to hold relics of St. Peter, St. Denis, and the Virgin's cloak.

They say no mortal could draw it free. Yet Rustechello placed his hand upon the hilt and felt a shiver of old power, as though the spirits of Roland and Arthur spoke from some ancient place. Whether he truly freed the sword or merely felt its weight in vision, none can say. But from that moment, his pen carried a fire unlike any other.

When he returned to France, Rustechello wove these visions into his great romance of Arthur, blending the real and the mythical, the sword of Roland and the sword of Excalibur, the Camino pilgrimage and the quest for the Round Table. His Arthur was not just a king of Britain — he was a symbol of Christian chivalry, a mythic standard for kings and knights across Europe.

Later, imprisoned in Genoa, Rustechello would share a cell with a restless Venetian traveller — Marco Polo. By candlelight, he recorded Polo's *Travels*, fusing fact and wonder, just as he had done with Arthur. His quill, once lifted in the Pyrenees, became the bridge between legend and history.

Centuries later, Christopher Marlow**e** and other dramatists would find in his work a seed of inspiration. What began as a king's commission and a pilgrim's road became a catalyst for storytelling across the ages, each retelling feeding the flame of the once-and-future king.

"Some swords are forged in fire. Others are forged in words." — *The Chronicle of Rustichello.*

Master of The Arts

In the mist between the two worlds, Merlin's prophecy still lingers with the hope of a rekindled, sometimes forgotten tale of Arthur, King and ruler of the magical kingdom called Camelot, for honourable knights of the Round Table, with quests for the Holy Grail, and a Lady of the Lake who holds Excalibur beneath the glassy waters, waiting for the hour when destiny will stir again.

So it was to prove time was by fate, not choice, that Rustichello de Pisa had made his way to Paris to seek an audience with the king. The bells of Paris had just begun to toll the hour when Rustichello da Pisa approached the Royal Palace. It was the year of our Lord 1279, and a cold wind swept through the great city, lifting the banners of lilies upon the palace towers. That day, the court of Philippe III — newly crowned King of France — was alive with ceremony and splendour. Nobles in embroidered robes, Templar knights in white mantles marked with the crimson cross, merchants, pilgrims, and poets filled the city like a river in flood.

Rustichello, cloaked in deep blue trimmed with gold thread, walked with the measured confidence of a man who carried more than coin in his purse. His boots, though travel-worn, struck the cobblestones with steady purpose as he approached the wide oak gates of the Royal Assembly Hall. Two Gardes du Corps du Roi, the King's bodyguards, stood flanking the gate — tall, broad men with polished breastplates and halberds shining in the winter light. They exchanged wary glances at the approaching stranger, for his bearing was neither that of a supplicant nor a servant.

"Stand and state your name and business," barked the elder guard.

Rustichello inclined his head with a slight bow, but his voice rang out with clarity.

"I am Rustichello da Pisa," he said. "Merchant of Venice, Knight of the Templar Order, and grandson of noble blood."

"Oui, oui," the porter at the gate interjected, waving a hand impatiently, his French accent thick. Then, with a mocking tone and broken English meant to unsettle, he added: "I did not ask you for your *family tree*, stranger. What is your profession? For no one passes these gates unless he is a *master* of some craft."

Rustichello let the question hang in the cold air for a heartbeat, then answered, "I am a merchant of Venice. But as to my profession, you may announce me to the King as *a Master of the Arts*."

This reply made the porter frown — not in anger, but in puzzlement. There was something in the stranger's calmness that unnerved him. Before the porter could speak again, Rustichello added firmly, "And tell the King this: if he has with him any man who claims to be master of all crafts at once, then I must have an audience with him."

The porter shifted uneasily. Around them, the bustle of the courtyard continued — trumpeters sounding, horses stamping, servants running with baskets of food and wine. Yet Rustichello stood unmoved, his cloak trailing like a banner behind him.

After a moment, the porter sighed and muttered under his breath, "By the saints, you're a bold one." Then louder, "Wait here. I will see what His Majesty says of this."

He disappeared through the great gate, leaving Rustichello beneath the towering arch, where tapestries depicting the victories of past kings swayed in the wind. A few curious squires whispered among themselves, pointing at the stranger in blue. One knight, passing by, cast him a measuring glance — the kind men of war reserve for other warriors.

Minutes stretched like hours., At last, the porter returned, his cheeks flushed with either haste or surprise. "The King has heard your claim," he said, half in disbelief. "He has sent his finest swordsman to test your hand — and his best chess master to test your mind. If you prevail, His Majesty will see you." Rustichello nodded slowly. A faint smile — more like the shadow of a smile — touched his lips. "Then let us begin," he said.

And so, beneath the archway of the Royal Assembly, with the banners of France fluttering above and the cold wind swirling around him, Rustichello da Pisa prepared to prove his worth not with begging or flattery — but with skill, mind, and legend.

Within the Royal Assembly Hall of Paris, the air shimmered with the warmth of torches and the scent of roasted meats and spiced wine. The high, arched ceilings caught the echoes of laughter, songs, and the clinking of silver goblets. Nobles and envoys from distant provinces gathered at long tables to honour the new King's coronation. Minstrels played at the far end of the hall, and pages hurried between guests like leaves scattered in a storm.

Upon the raised dais at the centre of the chamber sat King Philippe III, young but already marked by the weight of the crown. At his side stood his counsellors, among them knights of the realm, abbots of the Church, and men of learning who advised the throne. It was in this moment of festivity that the porter entered, bowing stiffly, hat pressed to his chest. Why do you disturb the feast?" Philippe asked, his tone steady but edged with curiosity. "Sire," the porter said breathlessly, "there stands at the palace gate a man who calls himself *Rustichello da Pisa*. He claims to be a merchant of Venice, a knight of the Templar Order, and — most strangely of all — a *Master of all the Arts*."

A hush fell upon the cluster of courtiers around the dais. A few exchanged sceptical smiles, others arched their brows. "Master of *all* the Arts?" repeated the King, leaning back on his throne. "A bold claim. Paris is full of braggarts during feasts. What sets this one apart?" "Sire," the porter continued, "he does not carry himself like a commoner. He speaks with assurance, demanding that the audience not see him as a petitioner but as an equal. He said, and I quote, *'If you have in your court any man who claims mastery over all crafts, then I must see him.'*"

A ripple of amusement and intrigue moved through the assembly. A noble chuckled into his cup. His sudden appearance drew the King's curiosity, and when he was informed of Rustichello's boast as Master of the Arts, He said, "Let us test him." Philippe declared. "If he claims mastery, then let him prove it. Captain, take your sword and meet him at the gate. Master Renaud, take your board and your mind. If this Rustichello is as skilled as he boasts, then I shall see him myself. If not—" He paused, the hint of a smile ghosting across his lips."—he will learn that kings have little patience for empty wind."

The court murmured its approval. Some whispered wagers were already being made — a few gold coins exchanged hands between knights eager to see the stranger humbled.

Sharp gaze. The King tapped his fingers on the armrest of his throne. Though young, Philippe III possessed a quick and discerning mind. "A man who speaks thus," he said at last, "must either be a fool or something far more dangerous. Tell me, who here doubts the worth of a true master?"

His eyes fell upon his Captain of the Guard, a broad-shouldered man known for his unmatched swordplay, and then upon the Court's Chess Master, a learned scholar from the south.

"Let us test him," Philippe declared. "If he claims mastery, then let him prove it. Captain, take your sword and meet him at the gate. Master Renaud, take your board and your mind. If this Rustichello is as skilled as he boasts, then I shall see him myself. If not—He paused, the hint of a smile ghosting across his lips. "—he will learn that kings have little patience for empty wind."

The court murmured its approval. Some whispered wagers were already being made — a few gold coins exchanged hands between knights eager to see the stranger humbled.

The Captain rose from his place, resting his gauntleted hand on the hilt of his blade. The chess master carefully folded his embroidered mantle, gathering his wooden board and carved pieces. Together they strode toward the great gate of the palace, the porter following in their wake.

Philippe III leaned forward on his throne and looked to his counsellors. "Let us see," he said softly, "if this man is a jester, or if he is a flame worth keeping."

Outside, the wind howled faintly through the courtyard. And there — cloaked in blue and gold — Rustichello waited, still as a statue, as destiny itself moved toward him.

The great oak gates creaked open, and through them stepped two men whose presence announced their rank even before a word was spoken.

First came the Captain of the Guard, a towering figure with a scar across his jaw and a blade at his side forged in Toledo steel. His boots struck the cobblestones with the rhythm of a war drum. Behind him, robed in dark green with a velvet cap, came Master Renaud, the King's chess master — a man of slight frame but sharp of eye, carrying under his arm an inlaid wooden board wrapped in crimson cloth.

Rustichello watched their approach in silence. He did not shift his weight nor bow his head. His cloak, heavy with the damp of winter air, fell around him like the wings of some patient bird of prey.

The Captain stopped just short of the archway. He looked Rustichello up and down with the practised eye of a man who had measured many before battle. "Stranger," the Captain said, his voice deep and edged, "His Majesty has heard your claim to be *Master of the Arts*. Here at the gate of kings, no man walks in on mere words. You will prove your worth — first by steel, then by mind."

Rustichello's eyes gleamed faintly, a spark behind calm waters. "Steel and wit," he replied. "A fair measure of a man."

The Captain drew his sword in one smooth, ringing motion. The courtyard quieted. A few squires had gathered at a respectful distance, whispering eagerly. The winter wind shifted, carrying the faint sound of music from inside the hall. Rustichello unbuckled the travel-stained leather strap at his side and drew forth a narrow blade — unadorned but deadly sharp, its edge kissed with light. Steel was drawn, a flash of silver sang through the still night air, and the two figures faced one another on status earned by some divine hand—poised, measured, eternal. There was no taunt, no haste, only silent promise, for when the final stole came, it would speak the voice of inevitability. There I moved. Rustichello disarmed the Captain of the Guards.

"The body may be swift," the chess master said, "but the mind reveals the man."

Rustichello seated himself without being asked, the faintest smile playing at the corner of his lips. Renaud made the opening move — a classical French gambit, bold and aggressive. Rustichello responded without hesitation, countering with a variation that made the older man's brows furrow in surprise.

The match unfolded swiftly. Renaud attempted a fork — Rustichello slipped away. A feint on the queen's flank — countered with a knight's dance. Within three measured moves, Rustichello had maneuvered Renaud's king into a corner. "Check," Rustichello said softly. Then after a single pause, "Mate."

The torchlight flickered as if stirred by the wind of that word. Master Renaud stared at the board in silence, then leaned back, a faint, reluctant smile curving his lips. "Remarkable," he whispered. "Not luck. Not a chance. Mastery." The Captain of the Guard placed a hand on Rustichello's shoulder, both as a gesture of respect and acknowledgment of victory. "The King will see you now," he said.

As the great gates swung open, Rustichello stepped through them not as a petitioner, but as one whose destiny had already begun to weave itself with the fabric of the realm. Behind him, the whispers of the court started to rise like wind in dry leaves: *"Who is this 'man?"* — *"A sorcerer?"* — *"A knight?"* —

The Porter was once more by the side of his King and eagerly announced the stranger's swordsmanship and chess-playing ability. Of swordmanship and chess-playing ability, he called it "Rustichello enclosure," which was what he had told the porter to say to the king. So he was invited in, and Rustichello, without a prompt from the King, sat himself upon the chair called the 'sage's seat,' which was kept for the wisest man.

The king overlooked Rustichello's impropriety in taking a place of importance in the assembly without asking. "So what is it that you want from me?" the king enquired. "I am seeking a position in your kingdom as a carpenter, for I am very skilled with my hands in that craft."

"May I enquire how you obtained that skill?" the King enquired. "I worked for a time as a carpenter's assistant, building 'Mary, the Holy Virgin' ship for the merchants' fleet and in designing and constructing storerooms for the Polo Brothers, Merchants in Venice."

The King paused for a while, head in hand, watching the strong man entertain. As if in passing, he replies to Rustichello, "We already have several boat builders, skilled carpenters, and master apprentices; I am in no need of another."

Patiently, Rustichello, watching the strength of the strongman bending a steel bar for the king's pleasure, states: "I am skilled as a blacksmith too." The King replies," We already have one of those; we don't need another." Rustichello suggests another of his capabilities. "I was a leader of a Knights Templar troop for several years, and I'm a professional warrior."

" We don't need one", says the King: Our strongman here, Omega, is our champion and was also a knight before I employed him."

Rustichello notices that the King was relaxing, no doubt having the savage beast within lulled by the steady play of the harpist. "I, too, am a harpist," says Rustichello. "But I also make up lyrics for the king's pleasure and melodies that will calm the mind."
The king responded, " I have a harpist, a poet laureate, and several musicians who can come up with melodies that inspire me. I am in no need of another."

The King watched as the strongman lifted a large boulder above his head and attempted to throw it like a shot put across the assembly room. "I am more than just a strongman, for I am a renowned warrior of great skill rather than mere strength," says Rustichello. The King responds: "I am content with whom I have."

"I am a great storyteller and writer of many romantic tales," says Rustichello. Then the King, a little impatient now, says, "As I have already indicated to you, I have poets, storytellers, and writers of renown. I am in no need of such services."

Rustichello now realises that actions speak louder than words, and he seeks to demonstrate some of his abilities. He watches as the King's champion, Omega, shows his strength by pushing a flag-stone so large that it took four oxen to move it there. The stone was only a part of a bigger rock nearby. Rustichello makes his way across the assembly floor and, with one hand, lifts the smaller stone, places it on top of the larger one. Then he picks up the harp and begins to sing a melody of his own composition that lulls the king and his guests into a temporary slumber, only to start a sad tune that makes everyone present weep. To finish his little set of songs, he sang a jolly tune, and the assembly laughed with joy.

It was then that the king recognised the many talents of the stranger and realised that someone so gifted could greatly assist his people against enemies. He dismissed the assembly after the feast and consulted with his chief advisers of the realm, instructing Rustichello to come to the throne room in an hour, after the king had returned from his afternoon nap. Of course, the king did not need sleep; instead, he used the time to devise a plan for his meeting with Rustichello in the throne room. The counsel, along with the theorists of the courts, advised the king to entrust Rustichello with the throne duties during his proposed visit to the far-off provinces of his kingdom in the coming six weeks. In the provinces, there was much unrest due to the influence of the Moors, who held territory formerly ruled by the Catholic Church and ultimately by the King of France himself. In addition, they were gathering troops on the borders of France, especially in Spain.

King Philippe recognised the man's extraordinary ability. Still, he first wanted to test the stranger before handing over the kingdom to him while he was away. He was eager to visit distant places to devise a plan to rid the kingdom of the Mongol threat.

Rustichello's Challenge.

So it was that King Philippe summoned Rustichello before him and asked about his need for service; "And how is it that a merchant of Venice, who would supposedly be wealthy in material possessions, would need to be in service in my kingdom?" He paused to continue: "Tell me what happened to inspire you to darken my door?' Rustichello then began to explain what tragedy had befallen him and to prove his need for employment at the king's bidding.

Rustichello began: "It was in 1260 that I finished building a storehouse for the travelling merchants Niccolò and Maffeo Polo. The brothers had been in business for many years before I started working for them, having established trading posts in Constantinople, Sudan, Crimea, and the western part of the Mongol Empire. As a duo, they reached modern-day China before temporarily returning to Europe to deliver a message from the then King of Mongolia to the Pope. At the time of their first journey to China, Niccolò left his young son behind in the care of his cousin's family, as his wife had died. The boy was to be educated through the Catholic system, learning Latin and Greek. I was assigned to help teach the young lad the ways of buying and selling merchandise, mainly supplied from Porto, Portugal. I was given responsibility over all of Europe for buying and exporting purchases from their trade centre in Venice. At this time, the two brothers had been living in the Venetian quarter of Constantinople, where they had their office.

However, I got word from a ship's captain that they were unwinding their merchant business and transferring northeast to Sudak, a city in the Crimea, as the city of Constantinople had become politically precarious, as you would no doubt be aware, my King, for you had been in service there for a time with your father during the war that followed."

When I received word again from another ship's captain that Constantinople was recaptured by the then ruler of the Empire of Nicaea, who had promptly burned and razed the Venetian quarter to the ground, capturing all Venetian citizens—who were then blinded—and those who did escape aboard overloaded refugee vessels bound for Venetian colonies died at sea. I was relieved to know my employers were safe in their new location, and I would have to grow the business in Europe at best, awaiting their return.

Rustichello then began to relate his night of the soul, which led him to the King's palace to seek employment for his majesty: "So it was I who travelled to Lisbon, Porto and other places along the Portuguese coastline; ports of call for the purchase of honey, animal hides, olive oil, figs and other commodities that I shipped from Portugal at Porto and transported also via the Port of Venice, destined for England at some of the English King's colonies."

" It was on such a trip earlier this year that tragedy befell me. Before leaving Venice, I had no one to handle my finances in my absence other than my wife. I had arranged with a Jewish moneylender to fund the journey and to provide ample funds to buy and trade commodities on my employer's behalf in my absence. I had given my wife power of attorney over all my worldly possessions and the authority to call on the Jewish moneylender to borrow money when needed. I mistakenly entrusted my love with an open line of credit to borrow as she willed, without imposing any restrictions. The Jewish bankers held as security in this instance a hold over all my possessions, including a family villa, a boat and a stable for my horses, of which I had paid in advance a stable hand to feed and exercise until my return."

Rustichello paused for a moment to catch his breath and requested a drink to clear his throat. The king ordered a servant to pour him a glass of wine, and once he had drunk it, composed himself, and continued:

" I was absent from Venice on my Master's behalf in Portugal for a period of three months before returning to Venice with a large quantity of supplies preordered and bound for England. In the meantime, my dear wife had taken a lover, squandered much of our wealth and used the line of credit to the full, left with her lover and my dearly beloved children to places unknown, leaving me with an empty house and a debt to the Jewish moneylender who began hounding me for his pound of flesh."

"After paying myself enough money to survive from the profit of those commodities destined for England, and giving what remained as an act of faith and goodwill to the Jewish moneylender who had a hold over my all, I got his agreement that he would not sell all that I once possessed until I could pay him back, giving me a period of three months from that date to clear the debt or he would sell all that I had accumulated. So, having an empty warehouse owned by my employer and no visible means of support, I have travelled here with the little that now remains. For I sold my horse on the outskirts of Paris to hire a coach to arrive at your house of assembly in the style to which I was formally accustomed, and I stand before you in the best of what I have left of clothing for my arrival here today to earn your trust and employment."
The King then related his need to travel to address his concerns about the dangers posed by the Moors holding territories on the

outskirts of his southern borders and in the North, where rebellious bandits held the Spanish Pyrenees. The Pope also destined him to drive the Moors out of Spain, particularly in the Iberian Peninsula. So he intended to leave Rustichello in charge, but with three provisions before this could take place: " You have but six weeks to complete three tasks on my behalf before my ultimate decision to appoint you as a warrior leader and leave you for a time in charge of my kingdom."

"Firstly, I want you to walk the Camino de Santiago from St. Jean Pied de Port at the base of the Pyrenees mountains to Santiago de Compostela in the far north of Spain on the Iberian peninsula. I want you to carry a burden representing my sin in the form of a bag of gold nuggets to lay at the altar in the Cathedral at the place where the ashes of St James reportedly lie."

Then the King, with his hand on his chin in a contemplative way, continued: "I will give you another small bag of gold to cover the cost of your journey. In addition, you may take from the sack of gold nuggets and give a nugget to any beggar along The Way, and stave off your Jewish banker for a time by sending him some of the gold from my bag, and whoever you consider is of a greater need for help than the sin I carry in my heart."

King Philip never disclosed what that sin was, nor did Rustichello think it any of his business other than to carry the burden of gold upon his own back for the sake of the King's relief of sin, the bag of gold, the majority of which was destined for the Santiago de Compostela Cathedral.

King Philip continues: "You have two other tasks to complete in the allotted time of six weeks before you return here. Firstly, under the cloak of being a pilgrim, continue your journey to the cape at

Finisterre and roam the wild coastline in this isolated part, going first to the village of Muxia. This path is less travelled than the fishing village of Finisterre, and whilst it has a sense of the wild sea and is the idyllic countryside for the heart of a poet such as yourself, you will remain as vigilant as a female servant in casting your net wide to see what stronghold the Moors have in the area. Then, on your way back to Finisterre, count the number of Moorish troops you encounter in your travels. Remember, you will appear as a pilgrim on the route, and if asked, you will answer 'that you wish to cast your sin into the sea' in the form of the shirt that you wear and pray at the little stone church built by St. James at Muxia in devotion to the Virgin Mary at the cliff face."

"And what is the third task, my King?" Rustichello enquires. " It is to return to me via the Camino lower route from Roncesvalles. For it is there I want you to extract from a rock the Sword of Roland that has been embedded there since the time of the great General Charlemagne, upon his retreat from Spain after wars with the Moors in the 700s. You, as a poet, would no doubt know of Roncesvalles and Valcarlos, where the battle of Roland took place. It has been immortalised in the 'Song of Roland.' It is the earliest of our French epic poetry from centuries ago."

Rustichello, not being a fan of French poetry, had to admit that he was unaware of the Roland Song but knew of the great battles of General Charlemagne. So, King Philip III, the newly crowned King of the Realm of France, took the opportunity to enlighten him.

Then the King once again reminded Rustichello of the three tasks he would have to complete for him, after which he would relinquish his throne for three months. Following that, he would appoint him as the leader of all his knights and military troops throughout the land. In addition, he would provide Rustichello with a purse to settle his debt to the Jewish moneylender, recover his earthly possessions—such as villas, horses, and stables—and give him enough money to trade again on behalf of the Polo brothers before they returned to Venice from their travels.

Of course, the King, being a man of clever plots, had not meant to release Rustichello from his duties to him that easily. He believed the young man didn't stand a chance of completing the third task of extracting the 'Durandal' Sword of Roland from its embedded place in the rock. No king, knight or warrior had been able to remove it in the last twelve hundred years since it was first buried there.

Rustichello was to learn, upon reading the Song of Roland, that he had relinquished the sword when his soldiers fell to the Moorish enemy. He was overpowered by the giant he had fought four days before, being defeated by him. When he fell, before his dying breath, he reportedly embedded the sword in a gap in the nearby boulder, intending to break it in two so it wouldn't fall into enemy hands. At his death, just as his faith in Jesus did, the sun darkened and the earth trembled. An earthquake briefly erupted, moving the rocks closer together, thus making the sword impossible to retrieve. It has lain on its side within the rock face at the Roncesvalles Pass ever since Roland took his last breath.

So Philip, King of France, sought to provide Rustichello with a history lesson about St. James preaching the gospel of Christ. He emphasised that living a divine life requires action, not just words. This idea is reinforced by the significance of Camino's journey in his quest for forgiveness. Additionally, he asked Rustichello to keep a daily journal of his experiences and prayers, requesting that he ask for forgiveness for the King's sins to no one on the Camino

Way. He also specifically asked that Rustichello assist other pilgrims struggling in their pilgrimage in the King's name.

The King had his scribe record all he told Rustichello because he believed it was vital that his instructions be followed precisely. The King was also eager to learn about any strange rituals, witchcraft, or mythical customs that influenced the people along this Camino route. He wanted to understand the mindset of those Rustichello met from Spain, their belief in a higher God, and whether they made offerings to the Catholic Church at the chapels along the way. Additionally, the King ordered all this to be documented in a book for future reference. He then dictated that any military details about Moor soldiers be excluded from the record. Such vital information was to be kept secret and only known to the King himself. The King then mentioned his desire for Rustichello to recover the sword of Roland, explaining its importance. He shared his great wish for Durandal, Roland's sword, and its role in defending the kingdom against enemies. He provided Rustichello with a journal to record his pilgrimage, along with a quill and ink to write down his daily experiences of The Way.

Then, as a final duty before starting the King's mission, the King sent Rustichello to his archivist's room to read the documents on the great General Charlemagne and the story of Roland. He wanted his charge to understand his mission, the path he must take: the mountainous route from St. Jean Pied de Port to Santiago, known as The Way of St. James. It was St. James who preached the message of Christ's suffering and sacrifice, emphasising that it was one thing to believe but that 'action speaks louder than words.' It was there that he read how Charlemagne, also called Charles the Great or Charles I, became the King of France in 768, the King of Italy in 774, and by 800, the first emperor in western Europe, since the collapse of the Western Roman Empire three centuries earlier. The documents detailed the expansion of the French state and its founding of the Carolingian Empire. It was Charlemagne who was considered to be the greatest ruler of the Carolingian Dynasty because of the achievements during what seemed like the very middle of the Dark Ages. To do this, he launched a 30-year military campaign from 772 to 804 that united Europe and spread Christianity. Charlemagne was engaged in almost constant battle throughout his reign, often at the head of his elite bodyguard squadrons, with his legendary sword "Joyeuse" in hand.

Rustichello read the accounts of his 46-year reign during which Charlemagne enjoyed unparalleled military victories, conquering most of Western Europe. From the Atlantic coasts of France to the west, the northern half of Italy to the south, modern-day Austria and Germany to the east, and north up to the North Sea, Charlemagne ruled it all. He never lost in battle but once, and it was under the leadership of his nephew Roland that the defeat transpired, for the young, brave warrior. Charlemagne's rear guard of war-weary soldiers were slaughtered when caught by surprise by a band of Basque bandits and Muslims when retreating through the narrow pass on the lower route of the Camino on that fateful day, August 15,778. Unlike Charlemagne's other hearty battles that he won, it was the defeat of Roland that was recorded in infamy. So before Rustichello continued reading Roland's famous struggle to the death, he summoned the court lute player to sing for him the immortalised La Chanson de Roland, The Song of Roland, the epic poem to get himself in a melancholy disposition and help him feel the sense of Roland's finale.

And so he set out — not as a courtier, but as a pilgrim. Cloaked in a simple brown mantle, a scallop shell pinned to his shoulder, he joined the stream of travellers walking the Camino Way from France to Santiago de Compostela. Along the road, he kept a diary, as the King commanded: recording the villages, abbeys, the faces of strangers, the whispers of Moorish movements in the hills of Navarra and the plains of León. He walked with merchants, monks, knights, and beggars, yet in every step there seemed to follow something older — a shadow of prophecy, as though Merlin's voice itself still lingered in the wind.

Weeks passed, and Rustichello reached the misted peaks of the Pyrenees on his return journey, where Roland's final battle had echoed centuries before. There, at the Roncesvalles Pass, the sun dimmed behind gathering storm clouds. Pilgrims often whispered that the memory of heroes and angels alike haunted the place.

He approached the mighty rock face where legend said Roland, mortally wounded, had driven his blade Durandal so that no enemy might ever wield it. The hilt still jutted from the stone like a shaft of light caught in the earth. Rustichello placed both hands on the sword. At that moment, the sky blackened, and a massive earthquake trembled through the valley. Stones tumbled loose from the cliffs; the wind wailed as if some ancient gate had been forced apart. Rustichello's grip tightened, and with a sudden, echoing crack, the blade came free- as if it had been waiting only for that moment, and for that man.

The pilgrims who witnessed it fell to their knees, some crying that it was miraculous, others whispering that the spirit of Roland had chosen him. Rustichello raised the word high, and for a heartbeat the storm ceased — the sun broke through the clouds like a blessing.

When Rustichello descended from the pass, Durandal hung at his side. Whether it was fact or Merlin's unseen hand at work, none could say. But the King's three commands had been fulfilled: hispers spread quickly through courts and cloisters alike — of the man who carried Roland's blade, of miracles on the Camino, and of a destiny entwined with kings, knights, and legend.

Be it the diary of Rostichello's journey of the Way, the manuscript writings he possessed, including Gregory of Monmouth's manuscripts of King Arthur and his Knights, the action in retrieving Durandal for King Philip III of France, or the murmurs of Merlin, we may never know. However, it was Rustichello, a great Master of Arts, who proved beyond a shadow of a doubt that the pen is mightier than the sword in his romantic account of the magic of the story of King Arthur and his knights. Be it the diary of Rustichello's journey along *The Way*, or the stories he drew from the ancient manuscripts of Geoffrey of Monmouth, it was clear that Rustichello carried with him not only a pilgrim's pack, but a scribe's imagination. Those old Arthurian tales became his template — the loom on which he wove a new legend for a new age.

His path to the Roncesvalles Pass, his fateful retrieval of Durandal for King Philippe III of France, and the whispered presence of Merlin's influence were not merely the stuff of chance. They became the threads of a story that would travel far beyond the peaks of Navarra.

And in the end, it was not the sword alone that endured. For though Durandal was forged of steel and glory, it was the pen of Rustichello that proved the pen mightier than the sword.

So it came to pass that when Rustichello de Pisa set his story of *King Arthur and the Knights of the Round Table* to paper, he also discovered among the scrolls of Geoffrey of Monmouth a lesser-known tale — a tale of Sultan Saladin.

Saladin, a noble warrior of the desert, had risen to power in the late 12th century. He fought with honour in the great Crusades, standing against King Richard the Lionhearted, and through strength and wisdom, he reclaimed Jerusalem for Islam. Yet even in victory, Saladin was known not for cruelty, but for granting peace to Christians and Muslims alike, holding the Holy City in balance until his final breath.

In the twilight of his years, Merlin — watcher across the mists of time — was said to have whispered this story into the mind of Geoffrey of Monmouth. Geoffrey, in turn, recorded it, though Rustichello chose not to include it in his romantic chronicle of Camelot.

Lest it vanish into the mist of lost imagination, this story is now set before you, the reader, for it is the tale of another singing sword.

As night settled over the desert encampment, Saladin withdrew from the counsel of his generals and sat alone beneath the vast canopy of stars. The weight of conquest, duty, and the suffering of nations pressed heavily upon his spirit. He had won many battles by strength of steel and brilliance of strategy, yet his heart felt no triumph in the echoes of war.

 In the stillness, he gazed toward the horizon where the sands met the moonlit sky, and he wondered if there existed a greater victory than dominion over lands and thrones. With a silent prayer for guidance, Saladin closed his eyes, unaware that the night would bring a vision destined to change not only the course of his own life, but the meaning of power itself.

The Sultan's Sword

One night, as the stars shimmered like scattered jewels above Damascus and the crescent moon — symbol of his faith — hung low in the sky, Sultan Saladin lay upon silken cushions, weary from endless campaigns. Sleep came softly, and with it, a dream.

The desert winds parted, their hot breath softening into a calm, fragrant breeze. Before Sultan Saladin stretched a hidden valley, veiled from mortal eyes, a place untouched by time. Silver rivers flowed like molten moonlight through fields of wild jasmine, and above, the stars burned with a brilliance known only in the realm of visions.

The ancient oaks that bordered the valley swayed without wind, their leaves whispering in tongues older than the great kingdoms of men. From their roots rose a faint mist, shimmering gold in the moon's crescent light. And there, at the valley's heart, stood a marble pedestal, smooth as if carved by the hands of angels and upon it rested a sword unlike any born of forge or flame. Its blade gleamed with a silver fire that neither flickered nor dimmed. In its steel, Saladin saw the reflection of two worlds — East and West — joined not by conquest but by shared destiny.

The hilt bore delicate inscriptions in Arabic, traced in filigree gold that caught the moonlight like flowing water. Interwoven with these, as though two tongues shared the same breath, were lines of Latin script, finely etched into the steel. The Arabic spoke of mercy, wisdom, and the will of the Divine, while the Latin whispered of kingship, honour, and the burden of destiny. Together, the two languages wove a single prophecy — a union of worlds long divided. One phrase shone brighter than the rest, as though alive with its own fire:

"Non gladio vincitur orbis, sed corde —
The sword does not conquer the world, but by the heart."

And beneath, in graceful Arabic calligraphy, was like water from the quills of angels, was inscribed:

”بالحكمة والنور تتوحد الأمم“
"By wisdom and light, the nations are made one."

The script itself seemed to breathe, its lines glowing faintly like embers beneath desert sand. Saladin's eyes lingered upon the final letters — a delicate crescent flourish — and at that moment, the hidden valley exhaled, as though it, too, had been holding its breath for centuries.

The wind stirred, warm and perfumed with the scent of cedar and myrrh. The rivers hushed, their mirrored surface turning to still glass. Every leaf and branch bent toward the pedestal, acknowledging the presence of a power both ancient and unbroken — as though the valley itself remembered the hand of Merlin who once passed through this place in another age. The oaks whispered in a tongue older than men, their leaves trembling in quiet reverence. The moon, a silver sickle, bathed the scene in a pale light that seemed to hold time still.

Saladin stood motionless, feeling the weight of the desert winds coiling around him. Where he stood was no ordinary place — it was a crossroads of worlds, where the breath of East and West mingled, where faith and myth shared a single language. He felt as though invisible hands guided him closer, step by deliberate step. He heard a voice from the singing notes in the sword speak directly to his soul..

The air shifted; warm desert winds mingled with the valley's cool breath, and in that meeting, Saladin felt the merging of two destinies. His people, the desert tribes — the bearers of the Crescent — and those across the sea beneath the Cross. The sword did not belong to one faith, nor one king. It was a covenant.

The branches of the great oaks lowered even further, their tips almost touching the ground, as though bowing before the moment. The river, running like a silver ribbon through the valley, stopped its flow, mirroring the stars perfectly, as if the heavens themselves leaned down to watch. The silence was complete — not empty, but filled with expectation.

And then — the sword sang. A single, clear note rose into the night. Not loud, but pure. It travelled up through the oaks, across the valley, and into the night sky, where it echoed like a call carried on the wind. Saladin knew it was not he who found the sword — it was the sword that had called him.

"بـالـحكمة والـنور تـتوحـد الأمـم" — *"By wisdom and light, the nations are made one."*
"Non gladio vincitur orbis, sed corde." — *"The sword does not conquer the world, but by the heart."*

A voice unfurled through the hum, soft and powerful as a tide:

"Salāh ad-Dīn… Keeper of the Crescent.
Step forth, for the blade remembers you.

Saladin approached. His shadow stretched across the marble like a veil of history. The moment his fingers brushed the hilt, the inscriptions flared — gold and silver entwined — and the valley shuddered as if waking from a thousand-year sleep.

His grip tightened. The sword yielded without resistance — it rose easily, as though eager to be held again. The forest sighed. The wind lifted. And Zemiatra — the Singing Sword — once forged in light and prophecy, chose its bearer anew.

 You are not the first… nor shall you be the last.
 This sword binds kingdoms as it once bound Arthur and his kin."

The Trail of the Stars

Then Merlin, in a playful way, interrupted the author of his words, defending Geoffrey of Mounmouth and indeed Rustichellos, for he did not tell this story to be opened up here but to savour it for another time.

To keep this author on track, he quickly summarised the Sultan's dream and the forging of the swords as a united front.

"For before his final awakening from his dream, Saladan saw, kneeling by the Lake, as the Lady's hand offered Excalibur. He saw Roland, crying Durandal's name to the mountains of France. And he saw himself, not as conqueror, but as keeper of a flame —a bridge between worlds.

The **voice faded** into the wind, leaving behind a single promise that settled in his heart like a seal:

All kings pass.
All swords sleep.
But legend endures…
If the heart remembers."

The valley exhaled. The stars seemed to pulse. And Zemiatra — the Singing Sword — rested in Saladin's grasp, a living relic bound to the destiny of men and myth alike.

"The air around the pedestal thickened, not with menace, but with reverence. The rivers grew silent, mirroring the sky as though heaven itself leaned in to listen. Then the sword began to hum — a sound soft as a distant choir, rising from the metal as if it possessed a living soul.
The voice that came was not spoken, yet it filled his mind like a clear bell: "Salāh ad-Dīn… Son of the Crescent. Keeper of the Desert's Law.
You stand where Arthur once was summoned, and where Merlin's shadow lingers.

Then the voice spoke softly once more:
" I am Zemiatra, the Singing Sword —
not forged by mortal hands, but born of oath and breath."

Saladin took a cautious step forward, his robes whispering over the marble floor. A warm wind swirled around him, lifting grains of gold dust from the earth. His hand trembled, not with fear, but with the gravity of destiny. As his fingers brushed the hilt, the inscriptions flared with light — Arabic and Latin burning in harmony. His mind was flooded with visions: He saw Arthur at the lake's edge, receiving Excalibur from the Lady's hand. He saw Merlin weaving spells of fate, his staff raised beneath the ancient oaks. He saw knights and kings of distant lands — Crusaders and Saracens, poets and pilgrims — all standing beneath the same moon. And, the blade's voice deepened, no longer a single note but a chorus—a harmony of distant echoes. The sound was unlike any mortal instrument, a music that seemed to speak in every language at once. It was not merely heard; it was felt, inside the bones, in the blood, in the breath.

Saladin stood beneath the silver canopy of the crescent moon, and the valley itself became a temple. The air swirled about him in slow, deliberate circles, carrying with it the scent of myrrh, cedar, and desert rain. The world beyond fell away.

And then, the vision came. The river before him turned to **a** mirror of light, and in its depths he saw figures emerging from the mists of time—a lake, still as glass. A Lady robed in water and starlight, her hand lifting a sword of equal radiance—Excalibur—toward a young Arthur. The boy's face was alight with both innocence and destiny, as if Merlin's breath was upon his crown. The image shifted. He saw Merlin himself, standing beneath ancient oaks, his cloak whispering in the wind. His eyes—those piercing, ageless eyes—looked directly at Saladin through the veil of centuries.

"All swords born of the old flame," Merlin's voice echoed, "are not meant for war alone. Zemiatra, Excalibur, Durandal… these are threads in the same tapestry. They pass from hand to hand, from king to king, where faith and courage are one."

Saladin felt the weight of the blade vibrate, as though it recognised these names, as though **it** remembered the hands of Roland and Arthur before his own. The vision swirled again: Crusaders crossing the sea beneath the banner of the cross—Saracen riders beneath the crescent moon. The vision swirled again: Crusaders crossing the sea beneath the banner of the Cross, Saracen riders beneath the Crescent, each believing themselves chosen by heaven. The sands of time shifted beneath their feet, and the blood of thousands mingled in rivers no one could claim as their own.

But in the centre of the battlefield, where smoke and steel clashed like storms, two figures stood apart — one bearing Excalibur, the other Zemiatra. Their blades did not strike but sang, two harmonies meeting in mid-air, creating a silence that rolled over the field like a sacred wind. Merlin's voice rose once more, woven through the music of the swords: "Two faiths. Two blades.One destiny.

This land was not made to be broken, but to be bound."

Saladin's grip on Zemiatra tightened. In the vision, the armies faded, leaving behind a single, vast and gleaming round table. Upon it sat no single king, but many thrones, their chairs unmarked by crest or colour. Above the table burned a single star — neither cross nor crescent, but light itself. Voice unfurled through the hum, soft and powerful as a tide that has risen since the world's beginning. It seemed to come from nowhere and everywhere at once — from the sword, from the stones beneath his feet, from the very breath of the valley:

"Salāh ad-Dīn… Keeper of the Crescent.

Step forth, for the blade remembers you.

You are not the first… nor shall you be the last.

This sword binds kingdoms as it once bound Arthur and his kin."

The words curled around him like threads of light, binding him not in chains but in the weight of destiny. As the sword's voice deepened, it became a chorus of echoes, as though a thousand voices from across ages joined in solemn agreement. The ground beneath the pedestal quivered, the air thickened, and the river fell utterly silent. Every leaf and branch of the valley leaned closer, listening. "Long before your crescent touched the sands," the voice continued, now echoing in both Arabic and Latin,

"I sang for Arthur beneath the mists of Avalon. Before him, I sang for Roland at Roncesvalles. And after you, others shall hear me — not for conquest, but to remind them that kingdoms are born not of fear, but of vision."

The inscriptions along the hilt blazed. The voice grew quieter now, closer, as though whispered directly into Saladin's ear: "If your hand lifts this blade in pride, it will turn to dust. If your heart lifts it in service, it will sing for you." Saladin inhaled deeply. Around him, the valley bowed, the moonlight gathering in a single shaft that struck Zemiatra's blade. His hand closed fully around the hilt. The sword rose easily, as though it had always known him. And with that motion came a flood of visions: And he saw himself, not as conqueror, but as keeper of a flame—a bridge between worlds. The voice faded into the wind, leaving behind a single promise that settled in his heart like a seal: "he had heard it before."

"All kings pass. All swords sleep. But legend endures…
If the heart remembers."

The sword's voice did not fade completely. It lingered — low and resonant — like the echo of a distant drum. The blade pulsed softly in Saladin's hand, and the air thickened with a scent like desert rain and cedar-wood. "I have slept through the rise and fall of empires," The voice murmured.

"Pharaohs have reached for me, knights have died for me, kings have prayed for me. But only those who listen — truly listen — awaken my song."

The blade began to hum, a sound not of steel striking steel, but of something alive. Symbols along the hilt shimmered — the Arabic calligraphy weaving itself into flowing verses of light:

"Strength without mercy turns to ash. Mercy without strength turns to wind.
But the hand that holds both… shapes destiny."

A flare of gold ran up the fuller of the blade, splitting into veins of light that arched outward into the valley. The wind rose in a slow spiral around Saladin, lifting the hem of his cloak.

"You are Salāh ad-Dīn," the voice continued, steady and commanding, "But before this night ends, you will become more than a name and a crown. You will become a memory. You will become a legend. But only if your heart can bear the weight of the song." The sword tilted slightly in his grasp, as if guiding rather than obeying.

The hum deepened, and now the blade sang — not words, but a sound that seemed to speak to the stars themselves. The valley answered in kind: rocks shivered, trees bent inward, and the sky itself brightened, a thousand hidden constellations burning into sight. Saladin's pulse matched the rhythm of the song. For a heartbeat, he was not alone — behind him stood the ghosts of warriors past, their faces carved of moonlight: Arthur, Roland, and nameless keepers before them. "The blade chooses not a king," whispered the sword, "But a keeper. Rule with the blade, and kingdoms will kneel. Guard with the blade, and time itself will listen." The glow narrowed, gathering into the point of the sword, which now hovered just above the earth. A single drop of light fell from the tip like a tear, striking the ground with a sound like a bell. "Your journey begins where conquest ends," the voice declared. "Now, Keeper of Zemiatra, step forward and hear the Trial of the Stars." The valley fell utterly still. The light under Sultan's feet formed a circle of runes, old as the wind itself. And the sword sang louder, calling him onward. The song of the sword swelled to a low, thunderous chord. The circle of runes beneath Saladin's feet began to rise, glowing like molten gold against the dark sand. The wind hushed. Even the stars above seemed to hold their breath.

Saladin lifted his gaze. Above him, the sky unfurled like a scroll, and from it spilled three rivers of light, each flowing down toward the circle where he stood. Then the voice came again — this time **not** just from the sword, but from the stars themselves.

"Three trials, Keeper of Zemiatra. Not of steel, nor fire, nor crown…But of *soul*. For a blade that sings must never rest in the hand of one who cannot hear its truth." The rivers of light wove themselves into three radiant figures — neither man nor ghost, but something in between:

The first, robed in crimson flame, held a broken banner. The second, cloaked in silver mist, carried a water bowl that never spilled. The third, crowned in shadow and starlight, bore nothing but a single word hovering over the radiant figure's palm: *"Choice."* The first figure stepped forward. Its voice echoed like steel drawn from a sheath:

"Trial One — The Sword of Power. All kings wield it. If given dominion over all lands, Salāh ad-Dīn, what shall you do? Rule with iron? Share with faith? Or burn it all to dust?"Saladin felt the blade tremble in his grasp — not with threat, but with anticipation. He saw visions flood around him: Cities kneeling beneath his crescent banner… Jerusalem in endless war… or in radiant peace. He spoke slowly, his voice steady as desert stone: "Power without mercy is tyranny. I would rule not to break nations, but to bind them to peace." The figure bowed once and dissolved into sparks.

The second figure glided forward, its robe of silver mist rippling like morning fog over a river. In its hands was a bowl of water, perfectly still, reflecting stars that had not yet been born. "Trial Two — The Sword of Wisdom. Knowledge is as sharp as steel, yet heavier than stone. You will see truths that will divide your heart:

Saladin stared into the water. In its reflection, he saw himself: Leading armies to victory, yet leaving villages in ruin, winning battles, yet losing the trust of allies. And through it all, he saw the voice of the sword, guiding him to more than triumph — to justice, balance, and mercy. He reached out, letting his fingers skim the water, not to disturb it, but to listen. "I will hold wisdom as my shield and mercy as my guide," He said. "I will act not for glory, but for the world that bears me." The silver mist rose into the sky, leaving behind a faint gleam of starlight that settled into the hilt of Zemiatra.

Finally, the third figure advanced, crowned in shadow and starlight. In its palm hovered the single word: "Choice."

"Trial Three — The Sword of the Soul. Every man faces this, Salāh ad-Dīn. Will you wield the sword for your own name, your own glory, your own kingdom? Or will you bear it as a living song, a covenant between worlds and peoples, a blade that binds legend to life?" The sword in Saladin's hand vibrated, its hum rising to a melody so evident it seemed the friends from foes, love from duty, faith from fear. Will you follow your heart, or the path that the world demands?"

After Saladin received the divine vision of his three trials—courage, wisdom, and mercy—he emerged from his reflection a changed man. He realised that true power was not measured by conquest alone, nor by fear and reputation, but by the balance of heart, mind, and justice. The vision impressed upon him that each moment of life was a test, and that time, once passed, could never be recovered. From that moment, Saladin applied disciplined mindfulness to his life. He devoted himself more fully to the care of his people, ensuring justice in the courts and fairness in taxation. Military campaigns were no longer just about glory; he sought to minimise unnecessary suffering, protect innocents, and honour truces. He cultivated scholars and doctors, built schools and hospitals, and encouraged religious tolerance in the lands he governed. The lessons of the vision stayed with him: For his courage was tempered by prudence; he learned to strike decisively but only when necessary.

Through courage, wisdom, and mercy, Saladin redefined what it meant to rule. He became a symbol not only of military skill but of moral authority. The people he governed and those who faced him in battle remembered him as a man who wielded power with conscience, whose name inspired respect rather than fear.

In his final days, Saladin reflected on these lessons. He taught it to his sons and generals, ensuring that his vision—the accurate measure of a life well lived—would endure beyond his passing. He died in Damascus in 1193, serene, his spirit untroubled, leaving behind a legacy of honour, justice, and a model of leadership shaped not just by triumph but by the trials of the heart.

According to certain later legends and poetic imaginings, Saladin's sword was said to *"sing"* in battle—not literally, but in the sense that it seemed to resonate with divine justice, courage, and honour. Every time it struck an enemy in righteous cause, the warriors and onlookers felt a sense of awe, as though the sword itself bore witness to the righteousness of its wielder. In mythic terms, the sword was more than metal; it was a conduit of virtue, embodying courage tempered by mercy, much like Saladin himself after his divine vision of the three trials.

In the quiet hours before dawn, Saladin stood atop the hill overlooking Damascus, the air thick with the scent of earth and the distant river's silver ribbon. In his hand, the sword felt alive, humming faintly, as if it carried a heartbeat of its own. The blade was no ordinary steel; this was a singing sword, a blade that knew the weight of justice, the echo of mercy, and the resonance of courage.

Legends whispered that the same spirit that made Durandal unbreakable and Excalibur a symbol of rightful rule flowed now through Saladin's hand. In battle, the blade would "sing" not with sound, but with resonance: a clarity of purpose that struck fear into the unjust and comforted the oppressed. Each movement was a lesson in wisdom; each parry, a testament to restraint. As he gazed over the city, he felt the presence of all the heroes who had carried swords like this—Roland, Arthur, the countless unnamed champions of justice. He understood that the sword's power was never in its metal alone, but in the virtue of the one who wielded it. A ruler without mercy would hear only silence; a heart without courage could never awaken its song.

He lifted the sword, imagining its voice reaching beyond the battlefield, through centuries yet to come. It sang of choices that mattered more than victories, of leadership guided by conscience rather than conquest. He recalled that the link between Roland's sword and his singing sword was symbolic: both symbolised royal *authority in* battle, a power that transcended mere physical strength. Durandal was indestructible, and Saladin's sword was "indestructible" in legend because it carried the weight of justice and divine guidance. And Arthur's Excalibur symbolises rightful sovereignty and the idea that power must be wielded wisely. Saladin's sword mirrors this theme: it is a test of character, not just a weapon, for all three swords wielded virtue and morality.

When Sultan Saladin grew old and his days of battle were behind him, Dur'Sal, the Singing Sword, remained ever at his side. Its song had guided him through victories and peacemaking alike, its relics shining with quiet power.

On the night of his passing, the Sultan lay in his chambers, surrounded by loyal companions. As he exhaled his final breath, Dur'Sal began to hum—a soft, mournful melody, rising like the desert wind through the palace halls.

The blade, luminous with the light of the relics within, gently lifted from its resting place, as if moved by the unseen. No mortal eye saw where it went, for legend holds that Dur'Sal vanished into the world of spirits, returning to the valley of dreams from which it first came.

Merlin's Cast of Characters.

So this author, now on a roll, realised that in his pursuit of the theme of Saladin and his singing sword, he would test Merlin's design rhythm. Thus, allowing the writer to follow a path of his own choosing in the Arthurian story, continuing to tell you, the reader, about his journey. This author felt it was indeed his duty to know of the Sultan's destiny in the three trials to test his wisdom in the rivers of the stars. It may be that time permits other writers to provide more detailed information about Saladin, as we know Rustichello chose not to include it. Different writers may later develop their Arthurian stories, exploring themes of duty, love, and chivalry. For now, it is here that the telling of Saladin and his three challenges, and the fate of his singing sword, is done, and I, the author, return to suss out Merlin's mind, to adventure to the next level of my Arthurian story that follows.

In the image of singing swords, the voice reaches beyond the battlefield, through centuries yet to come. It sang of choices that mattered more than victories, of leadership guided by conscience rather than conquest. In that melody, we see the lesson for every age: the accurate measure of power is the courage to act rightly, the wisdom to choose justice, and the mercy to forgive even when it costs.

However, for centuries, despite his best efforts, Merlin fell on hard times, and a sense of madness set in as he retreated into the depths of a deep, dark forest, becoming a wild man. For centuries, the forest held him. Its roots curled around his sleep, its moss wrapped his mind like a green shroud. The great magician, Merlin, had walked too far into the realm between reason and vision. He had seen too much of man's folly and too much of time's wheel. And so, like a storm breaking itself on the cliffs, he had retreated into the deep wood where no king's trumpet could reach him.

They called it madness. The truth was far stranger.

In his solitude, Merlin spoke to trees older than empires. He argued with ravens about destiny. He listened to rivers recite prophecies. For centuries, time wound itself around him like ivy. The world outside rose and fell, but in the forest, the magician waited—watching history through the green veil.

Then, one night, as the stars aligned as they had in the Age of Arthur, he stirred. The old powers whispered, *"It is time."*

Merlin opened his eyes, and the forest itself shivered. He was no longer the sage of Camelot alone; he was the keeper of memory, the archivist of myth. He stepped from the trees and found not knights nor kings, but *a writer*—a mortal at the edge of the modern age, pen trembling like a sword.

"So," Merlin said, his voice a mixture of thunder and oak, "You would write of Arthur again. Then you must face the living memory of myth." He raised his staff, and the mists parted. From the haze, the characters of his legend emerged one by one: Arthur Pendragon, the once and future king — noble, flawed, destined to unite and to fall. Guinevere, queen of light and sorrow, her love a blessing and a wound. Lancelot, the knight whose valour could not shield him from the fires of forbidden love. The Lady of the Lake, her eyes deep as eternity, holding Excalibur like a shard of fate itself. Morgana, shadow and mirror, the counter-song to Camelot's bright dream. The Knights of the Round Table, each a star in a constellation that burned brilliantly before the night that Merlin turned to the writer.

"To speak their names is to summon them. To tell their story is to walk the fine line between glory and ruin. Camelot rose on the promise of a perfect world—and fell on the frailty of human hearts." The vision unfolded: Excalibur rising from the lake, Arthur crowned, the Round Table shining, then cracks forming like frost on glass—Lancelot and Guinevere's secret, Mordred's betrayal, and at last, the fall of Camelot, where the dream shattered but did not die.

Merlin's eyes burned with an ancient fire.

"My madness," he whispered, "was not forgetfulness. It was waiting. Every age needs its Arthur. Every heart must choose between the shining dream and the dark truth beneath it. If you write this tale, you are not just a storyteller. You are the next keeper of the flame."

It was then I realised that he was not just talking about those storytellers of the past; he was directing his thoughts also to me.

The forest wind howled, and leaves spiralled like ancient banners. Then—Merlin vanished. Only the echo of his laughter lingered, a sound like the rustling of pages older than time itself. The writer, pen trembling, realised: the myth of Camelot isn't locked in the past. It breathes anew each time someone dares to tell it.

Merlin would create in the mind of a dreamer of myths and storytelling, a cast of characters, followed by the story of Camelot. They would come to Geoffrey of Monmouth like figures stepping from shadow into firelight. First would come Arthur Pendragon, the boy who would be king. Hidden from birth, chosen by destiny, he drew a sword from stone and bound a land together beneath a single crown. Around him would rise the shining towers of Camelot, a kingdom built not on fear but on chivalry and hope.

By Arthur's side, and that of the scribe, would stand Merlin, wise and strange — a prophet, a seer, a bridge between the old world of enchantment and the new world of kings. It was Merlin who guided Arthur's hand, Merlin who spun the web of destiny.

Then, to bring a little magic into the feeling of his enchantment would come Guinevere, the queen of unmatched beauty, whose heart carried both love and sorrow. She was the light of Camelot and the shadow at its edges. Beside her would ride Sir Lancelot, the perfect knight — brave, noble, and bound by a love that would burn brighter than loyalty.

From the north rode Gawain, steadfast and proud, Arthur's loyal nephew. And behind him, Galahad, the purest of knights, destined to seek the Grail. Around them would gather the noble fellowship: Percival, Kay, Bedivere, Tristan, and Bors — the Knights of the Round Table, sworn to serve honour above all.

But not all who walked in Camelot's shadow would be of goodwill. Out of the mist would come Morgana le Fay, enchantress and half-sister to the king — beautiful, dangerous, and woven of the same magic that flowed through Merlin himself. She would be both ally and adversary, love and doom.

And from darker roots Mordred, born of blood and betrayal — the usurper, the shadow Arthur could not escape. In his eyes burned the end of Camelot.

Yet even beyond mortal hearts, the myth deepened. From the still waters rose the Lady of the Lake, shimmering and eternal, who placed the sword Excalibur into Arthur's hands. And far away, beyond mist and mortal sight, lay Avalon, the Isle of Dreams — where swords do not rust, and kings never truly die.

Thus was the cast set — heroes and traitors, queens and sorcerers, knights and shadows. And that would be the template that Merlin would weave until Geoffrey took up his quill, and the whisper would become words, and the words would become legend. And so many Knights would come from all points of the compass to live the dream that was Camelot. And so Camelot would be born… not in stone alone, but in the breath of story. For the Kingdom of Camelot, in all the dreamings of Merlin, never looked brighter than at its height, but before the fall. Merlin appeared to Arthur as a final warning of what was to come.

The fire burned low in the Hall of the Round Table. All about, the great oak pillars creaked softly, as though the bones of Camelot itself shifted in uneasy slumber. Rain swept against the high windows, whispering in the darkness.

Merlin stood apart from the circle of chairs, his cloak gathered like storm clouds about him. In his hand, his oaken staff pulsed faintly, as if remembering secrets older than the stones of Camelot. Arthur sat alone at the head of the table, his crown resting like a weight of iron rather than gold.

"Speak," Arthur said softly, his voice carrying in the hollow of the hall. "You have walked in shadow, old friend. What did you see?"

Merlin's eyes, deep as the roots of Brocéliande, flickered toward the empty chairs of the knights. The Round Table gleamed with the light of a hundred candles, each flame reflected in the polished surface like stars in dark water.

 "I have seen," Merlin began, "the flaws that lie not in stone, but in men. You have built a kingdom on courage and noble hearts. But even the strongest oak cracks from within."

Arthur straightened in his chair. "Name them."

Merlin moved slowly, like a storm crossing a moor, his voice falling to a whisper that seemed to fill every corner of the chamber.

"First, there is Lancelot," Merlin said. "A blade without equal. A knight whom poets will praise until the rivers turn to dust. But his heart is already chained. Not by a foe's hand… but by the queen's eyes. Love, Arthur. It will not pierce your armour, but it will split the foundation beneath your feet."

Arthur's hands clenched on the arms of his chair. Merlin's gaze held steady.

"Then there is Gawain. His loyalty burns like the noon sun, but so too does his temper. Pride will be his horse, rage his sword, and one day, both will ride faster than his reason."

"And Galahad—the purest among them. So pure, in truth, that he stands apart even when among brothers. Holiness is a lonely fortress. A heart too high cannot hear the cries below."

"Percival is a lamb wandering in a den of wolves. His innocence will be both his shield and the crack through which darkness fell when Merlin's voice changed. The room grew cold. "And then,"

Merlin whispered, "there is the shadow born of your own blood. Mordred."

The candles flickered, and Arthur's breath caught in his throat. Sharp of mind. Cunning as the serpent beneath the apple tree. A wound wrapped in a smile. His treachery will not come as a stranger, Arthur—it will come wearing your own face."

A long silence followed, broken only by the hiss of rain against the stone.

Arthur rose, slow as a man bearing a mountain on his shoulders. "And what then, Merlin? Am I to cast out my knights? Shatter the Table before the first crack forms?"

"Bors… wise and balanced, yet torn between heaven and earth. A man with two masters is a man with none. He will see the end, Arthur. But he will not stop it."

"Tristan walks with a melody in his heart—a love song fated to end in sorrow. He will follow love as others follow duty, and that path leads not to Camelot… but away from it."

"Kay, your foster brother. Loyal, yes. But the tongue of a bitter man can wound more deeply than the sword. Envy is a small flame, but it spreads quickly through dry timber."

Arthur lowered his eyes at that, for he loved Kay as one loves the memory of childhood.

"Bedivere's flaw is a quiet one. A good heart that trembles at the edge of destiny. When the final choice comes, his hand will falter. And though he will find courage in the end, it will come too late to mend the breaking."

"Geraint loves too fiercely. He will make a fortress of his heart around his lady—and like all fortresses, it will imprison him as well."

"Gareth… bright, young, believing the world is noble because he himself is noble.
 But war is not a song, Arthur. It is a dirge. The boy's dream will meet the iron of the world."

"Palamedes will forever chase what cannot be caught. The questing beast is his shadow. Some men are born to seek, not to find. His restlessness will keep him far from the battles that matter most."

Merlin's staff struck the floor once. The sound echoed like a distant bell.

"No," he said. "For flaws are not yet ruin. They are warnings.
 The oak does not fall at the first whisper of rot—but if the king ignores the whisper, the storm will find it."

Merlin moved toward the great doors, his shadow stretching long across the floor. "Love them, Arthur. Guide them. But never forget what I have told you tonight. For the doom of Camelot will not come from outside its walls. It will be born *around this very table*."

And with that, Merlin was gone—leaving Arthur alone with the flames and his gathering storm of thoughts.

Seeds of the Lotus.

Let us go back to the beginning…Before the knights, before the sword in the stone, before the White Cross of the Templar Order ever flew — there was a night of quiet fire, a forest heavy with mist, and an old enchanter walking beneath the yew trees.
Seed of an Oak.

It was the winter solstice in the early 12th century when Merlin came to Geoffrey of Monmouth. Geoffrey — a scholar, cleric, and chronicler — was alone in his cell, bent over parchments, seeking the history of kings that would make sense of a fractured land.
England was torn between Norman overlords, Saxon memory, and older Celtic whispers. Geoffrey sought facts, dates, battles — but the truth he longed for lived not in ink but in legend.

The fire in the brazier flickered low when the door did not open, but the air itself bent. A soft wind carried the scent of wet earth and hawthorn, and Geoffrey looked up to find a figure standing in the shadows. The wild-looking stranger wore no crown, yet his eyes burned brighter than the coals. His beard was silvered like moonlit frost. Ravens circled silently above the roof.

"Who are you?" Geoffrey whispered.
"A memory," Merlin said. "And the gardener of a seed."

Merlin sat opposite him, though the chair had not been there a moment before. He leaned forward, voice low and patient, as if speaking not to one man but to all who would ever tell stories.

"You scratch at the past like a sparrow at a stone," he murmured. "But the past is not enough. Kingdoms need dreams. Kings need something greater than themselves to follow."

From beneath his cloak, Merlin drew a small round disc of yew wood, inscribed with a circle and twelve points — the first image of what would become the Round Table.

 "Write of a king who binds sword and mercy," Merlin said. "Write of a land where the just and the mighty are the same.
Write of knights who rise not for plunder, but for a light no hand can touch."

Geoffrey trembled. The words did not sound like suggestions — they sank into him like roots into soil. He felt as though the quill in his hand was no longer his own.

"Arthur," Merlin whispered. "His name shall be Arthur.
He will bear a sword forged in hope.
His court shall sit at a round table so no man stands above another.
His queen will be beloved—his knights, flawed but brave.
And in the end, his kingdom shall fall… so it may rise again in memory."
The next morning, Geoffrey's quill moved as if guided by unseen hands. He began writing the *Historia Regum Britanniae — The History of the Kings of Britain*. And there, between battles and bloodlines, the figure of Arthur emerged: not merely a king of men, but an idea — the seed Merlin had planted.

He wrote about: The Sword in the Stone, which only the true king could draw, based on prophecies told to him by Merlin that would prove to be mysterious and timeless. He described a noble company of knights who ride in Arthur's name and envision a future for a kingdom called Camelot—a bright dream of law and order in what was, at the time of Geoffrey's writing, a brutal world. A place where noble knights would come from far and wide to sit at a

Round Table where noble deeds would be discussed and acted upon for the sake of Camelot, and all that rallied under its banner, in that bright stream of order for king and country.

What Geoffrey could not know was that this story, once told, would not stay still. It would grow, carried by troubadours and monks, knights and dreamers, until it reached every corner of Christendom.

And so Merlin returned to the forest, as he always did. He knew kingdoms would rise and fall. He knew men would twist myths to their ends. But the seed was planted — and seeds endure. "When kings fall," he whispered to the trees, "the dream will rise in another man's hand. And another. And another." And through Geoffrey, through Camelot, through the Templars, troubadours, secret orders, and modern dreamers… the seed lives still.

The 12th century was a restless time. Christendom expanded eastward; the Holy Land drew kings, crusaders, and pilgrims. Among those who journeyed to Jerusalem were nine knights, poor in coin but rich in faith and purpose. Their leader was Hugues de Payens — a man who believed not merely in war, but in the defence of the sacred. They made a simple vow: To protect pilgrims on the roads. To live as brothers. To serve something greater than themselves. And so, beneath the shadow of Solomon's Temple, the Order of the Poor Knights of Christ and of the Temple of Solomon — the Knights Templar — was born.

So, dear reader, indulge me a little while I bring to your attention some historical facts regarding the Knights Templar. The distinction between fact and fiction regarding the Knights Templar will shed more light on Merlin's vision, which he planted in the mind of the writer Gregory of Mounmouth during those troubled years of the Crusades, wars, and rumours of wars. In fact, the British Empire was in chaos and disharmony in England at the time, giving more credence to the story.

The oath of the Templar knights dates back to the First Crusade. Their oath was binding by honour, duty to the Pope, King and country: "A Templar Knight is truly a fearless knight, and secure on every side, for his soul is protected by the armour of faith, just as the armour of steel protects his body. He is thus doubly armed and needs fear neither demons nor man."

But the men were not only stirred by the Gospels. In the years before, Geoffrey of Monmouth's stories of Arthur had spread across Europe like wind through tall grass. Troubadours sang of Camelot in the courts of France, England, and the Rhineland. The image of Arthur's Round Table — a fellowship of the brave and the pure — caught the imagination of knights who longed for something nobler than plunder.

They heard of: Arthur's brotherhood, bound not by blood but by oath—the Round Table, where rank and wealth faded before honour. The Grail Quest is a sacred mission beyond the reach of earthly kings. And they began to see their own vows reflected in that myth. Though they bore swords and shields, they believed themselves defenders of a greater ideal.

"Camelot was a story," whispered one Templar chronicler, "But God gives stories to men so that they might build them upon the earth." The red cross upon their mantles became for some a new Excalibur — a symbol of a holy mission, sharp as steel, radiant as a legend.

In mythology, long before the Order of the Templar Knights took hold, St. James reportedly led Christians in the Battle of Clavijo in 844 AD. The legend says he appeared as a warrior on a white horse to help the Christian army defeat the Moors, approximately 800 years after his death. The myth tells of a band of knights who followed him into battle, draped in white with a red cross on their shields. It may be from this mythical tale that the Order of Santiago, a Christian military religious order of knights, was founded about 1160 in Spain for the purpose of fighting Spanish Muslims and protecting pilgrims on the way to the shrine of St. James of Santiago de Compostela on the series of routes that became known as the Camino Way. The Knights of Santiago spread throughout Europe, adopting the mantle of the Knights of their province and embodying the same humility, honour, and obedience as envisioned by the founders of the Templar Knights. A similar code of honour persists, as Merlin envisaged it through the mind of Godfrey of Monmouth.

So far from the East, deep in the forests of Britain, an old figure watched. Merlin, who had long since withdrawn from the affairs of kings, walked again beneath the oaks. The stories he had seeded now bore fruit in the form of real men.

He spoke to the wind: "A myth is a map. Some follow it to the stars. Some follow it to war. Let us see where this river runs…"
Merlin knew that every light casts a shadow. The Templars embodied both: The idealism of Camelot — honour, unity, spiritual purpose. And the danger of power, wealth, secrecy, and pride.
Just as Arthur's dream had risen and fallen, so too would the Templars'—for no ideal can live unguarded forever.

As their influence grew, whispers began to swirl: They searched for relics beneath Solomon's Temple. That they carried secret knowledge west, that among their treasures lay a cup, a stone, or a scroll tied to the *Grail of Arthurian myth*. Whether truth or legend, the stories intertwined like vines, with the Templar Grail becoming inseparable from the Arthurian Grail. And the Round Table's ideals bled into the real-world order of warrior-monks. Many a chronicler — consciously or not — saw the Templars as heirs of Camelot's dream.

But just as Merlin had whispered to Geoffrey: "Even golden ages fall." The Templars rose in power — vast lands, fleets, banks, secrets. Kings who once praised them now feared them. And on a cold October dawn in 1307, Philip IV of France struck. The Templars were arrested, accused of heresy, tortured, and burned.
In that fire, their order died in flesh — but lived on in myth.

For legends do not burn efficiently. The Arthurian seed that had inspired their beginnings returned to the soil of story, ready to grow again in other forms — in Freemasonry, in secret brotherhoods, in modern imagination.

Far away, in a forest older than memory, Merlin smiled. "I planted a story in the heart of one writer," he whispered. "And the story grew into men. And the men fell, as all do. But the *dream*… the dream survives."

The dream of Camelot became the soul beneath the steel of the Templars. And the Templar legacy became **a** modern grail — endlessly sought, endlessly retold. Because myths are not cages.
They are seeds, waiting for the next mind to receive them.

The first seed Merlin planted grew into Geoffrey's *Historia Regum Britanniae*, and from there into the spirit of the Knights Templar. But when the Templar Order burned, the story did not die. It descended into the soil of memory—dark, secret, and powerful.

The year was 1314. In the flickering light of a Parisian square, Jacques de Molay, the last Grand Master of the Templars, was led to the stake. The executioner thought he was burning a man. But what he burned was the previous public face of a myth. As the flames rose, witnesses swore the old knight did not scream. He spoke—a curse on kings, a call to God, and a whisper to the future. In some tellings, he also spoke of a treasure that could not be found with hands. The Templar gold could be seized. But their story, already tied to Arthur and the Grail, scattered like glowing embers on the wind.

After their fall, legends spread like ivy over ruined stone: Some said the Templars had hidden a sacred vessel—the Grail—in remote lands. Others claimed they fled to Scotland, or to the Pyrenees, or sailed across unknown seas. Still others believed their true legacy was not treasure at all, but knowledge—a code of chivalry and mystical lore older than kings.

And as Europe entered the long night of wars and plagues, these whispers intertwined with Arthurian songs sung by troubadours. Camelot, once a literary vision, became a ghostly memory of a lost age of honour. The Templars became its secret heirs—rightly or wrongly.

Far away, deep in the green shadows, Merlin stirred. "I told Geoffrey," he whispered to the trees, "that Arthur's kingdom must fall so it might live in story. Now the Templars, too, have fallen. The pattern holds." Merlin's magic was not the magic of fire or lightning. It was the magic of narrative — a power that outlives men, kingdoms, and cathedrals. And just as Camelot's ideals once inspired the Templars, the Templar fall gave Camelot a new face: No longer just a court of knights — now a hidden fellowship, a veiled order, a questing brotherhood that could rise again when the world needed it.

In the timeless forest, Merlin stood by the riverbank, staff in hand, watching the currents. "I planted a single story," he murmured, "and it became a kingdom. The kingdom fell, and became a brotherhood. The brotherhood fell, and became a song. The song travels now on every wind. That is how legends conquer time."
He turned toward the dark wood, disappearing as he always did, leaving only the echo of his words and the rustle of leaves. Camelot was never only a place. The Templars were never only an order. The Grail is not merely a cup. They are one mythic river, flowing from Merlin's whisper through history's storms, feeding the imagination of every age that hungers for honour, courage, and a light that power cannot extinguish.

"The sword rusts," Merlin once said, "But the story shines forever."

"All these men were of noble birth, and their life stories would fill volumes of books. Much like the mythical story of King Arthur and the Knights of the Round Table, these knighted gentry were dedicated to building an army of Knights. Their initial duties were to launch a fundraising campaign, seeking donations of money, land, or noble-born sons to join the Order. The implication that many contributions would help to defend the city of Jerusalem attracted many noblemen and peasant labourers to be trained as Knights. The Order became known as the Poor Fellows; Soldiers of Christ of the Temple of Solomon, which was eventually shortened to Knights Templar. Little was heard of the Order for the first nine years, until 1129, when it was officially sanctioned by the church at the Council of Troyes. It was then that they became well-known throughout Europe. The Order, from its foundation, was heavily criticised by those of religious faith who could not agree with the concept of religious men carrying swords.

There was a catalyst to the power that was to become the Way of the Templar. The papal bull 'Omne Datum Oprimum', issued by Pope Innocent III in 1139, decreed that the Templar Knights could pass freely across any border, owed no taxes, and were subject to no authority except that of the Pope, thereby granting them even more power. The Knights' influence by then had spread to France, England, Scotland, Spain, Portugal, and Malta. The Templars had become the elite fighting force of their day, highly trained, well-equipped and highly motivated. One of the tenets of their religious order was that they were forbidden to retreat in battle unless outnumbered three to one by a commander's order or if the Templar flag went down.

Initially, an order of poor monks with an official papal sanction, the Templar Knights took an oath of poverty. As more and more free men became Knights, they continued to donate their cash and property to the Order. The Templars were trusted with large sums of money and land to protect. The Knights Templar became known as the safest 'bank place' in Christendom. They developed an international banking infrastructure, using letters of credit and promissory notes to transfer funds over long distances. Many Pilgrims visited the Templar Castles and entrusted all their wealth and business controls to the Templars to safeguard it for them.

The Order's power grew substantially because the majority of its infrastructure was devoted not to combat but to economic pursuits. The Knight's involvement in banking grew over time into a new form of currency. The transition from fighting to finance changed the course of the initial founders and the Templar mission. Their sometimes usurious practices led to controversy within the Church at large. The Templars cleverly sidestepped the Church Rule, which forbade lending money for a return of interest, by stipulating that they retained the right to receive interest on property loans. Since they were not allowed to charge interest, they charged rent instead.

Meanwhile, the Moors under Saladin caused many Knights' deaths in battles against his troops to seize Christian lands. Enter Richard the Lion-Heart, King of England and leader of the Third Crusade, made up of his own Knights with the aid of the Knights of the Templar throughout Europe. They, in a short, swift, and decisive campaign, delivered a series of powerful blows against Saladin and recovered much of the Christian territories.

Richard relied heavily on the Templars and saved the Holy Land. Whilst the power struggle between Christians and Muslims raged for many years, Islam gained the upper hand and the Templars were forced to make their headquarters on the island of Cyprus, having lost their power base in the Holy Land. In a final attempt to regain the Holy Land in 1298, the Templars lost a brief encounter in Armenia against the Muslims. Soon, the fortress of Roche-Guillaume in the Belen Pass, the last of the Templars' strongholds, was lost to the Muslims. Another attempt to regain territorial control was won near Torosa, but soon lost. In Cyprus, the Templars controlled considerable financial resources, yet the Order lacked a clear purpose, despite still holding enormous economic power.

Their reign ended when King Philip of France feared the Order of the Templars' power. The Templars had a castle in southern France and also took over the island of Cyprus, forcing King Henry I of Cyprus to abdicate in their favour. The Templar order's control of property made Philip uneasy, as he had inherited land in Champagne, France, a historic Templar headquarters, a few years earlier.

The Templar, institutionally wealthy, paid no taxes and had a large standing army that, by papal decree, could move freely across European borders. Philip had inherited an impoverished kingdom from his father and was deeply in debt to the Templars. King Phillip's motives, being mostly personal, political and religious, missed the opportunity to disband the Order. He discovered the rituals of the Knights and, with this knowledge and Vatican support, put into play the downfall of the Templars.'

"There were five initial charges lodged against the Templars. The first was the spitting on the cross during initiation into the Order. The second was their stripping of the man to be initiated, and the third was kissing of that man by the Preceptor on the navel, posterior and mouth. The third was telling the novice that unnatural lust was lawful. The fourth was that the cord worn by the novice day and night was consecrated by being wrapped around an idol in the form of a bearded human head. The fifth point was that Templar Priests did not consecrate the host during the celebration of Mass.

The outrages were great, and fairy tales began to emerge. One such charge was that the Templars worshipped an idol of a cat and a head with three faces—further charges of denying Christ by spitting and urinating on the cross, and of devil worship of Baphomet. Even though the confessions had been produced under duress, they caused a scandal in Paris, with mobs calling for action against the blaspheming Order. Of the 138 Templars questioned in Paris over the next few years, 105 of them 'confessed' to denying Christ during secret Templar initiations, 103 confessed to 'obscene kissing' being part of the ceremony, and 123 said they spat on the Cross.

Throughout the trial, there was never any physical evidence of wrongdoing, no independent witnesses and the only proof obtained was from the confessions induced by torture. Pope Clement issued a bull that instructed all Christian Monarchs in Europe to arrest all Templars and seize their assets. Most Monarchs simply did not believe the charges, but proceedings were started in England, Iberia, Germany, Italy and Cyprus against the Order.

The dominant view is that Philip, who seized the treasury and dismantled the monastic banking system, was jealous of the Templars' wealth and power. Frustrated by his enormous debt to them, he sought to seize their financial resources himself by bringing false charges against them. It is widely accepted that Philip made up the accusation and did not believe any of the Templars were party to such activities.

Many of the Kings and nobles, who had been supporters of the Knights up until then, finally dissolved the Order in accordance with Papal command. Most were not as brutal as the French. In England, many were arrested and tried, but not found guilty. Much of the Templar property outside France was transferred by the Pope to the Knights Hospitaller on the Camino Way, and many of the surviving Templars were accepted into that Order. They served as guardians of the Pilgrim until their dying day.

Knights, Grail & Ark

The Order of the Temple Knights continued to exist in Portugal by simply changing its name to the Order of Christ. This group was believed to have contributed to the first naval discoveries and was led by Prince Henry the Navigator for twenty years until his death. Other Templars simply joined other similar orders, and there are still questions of what became of the thousands of Templars across Europe and of the 15,000 Templar Castles erected during their reign. The mystery of the many plans and designs created by the Templar still stands today, including the great Caravel warships built during the Spice Wars.

The extensive archives of the Templars' feats may hold the secrets of the Holy Grail, the Ark of the Covenant, and a vast treasury of gold. The story is of knights who, on 18 ships, carried it to prevent it from falling into French hands during Philip's reign. The Templars took with them vast wealth and excellent knowledge as they left for greener pastures, keeping their wisdom and power intact.

The night was moonless, the stars shrouded behind a veil of cloud. Upon the restless sea, eighteen ships cut through the black waters like silent blades. No banners flew. No torches flared. Only the whisper of sails and the breath of fate carried them forward. On their decks stood the Knights Templar, faces hidden beneath white cloaks marked with the crimson cross. They had not only gold and relics… but the last light of their Order. Behind them, the Old World burned with treachery. Ahead lay only the mists of legend.

Then came the fog — thick, silvery, unnatural. The helmsmen swore they heard a voice in the wind, Soft as the turning of a page, ancient as the earth. *"Follow the star beyond all maps,"* the whisper said. *"For where the mortal sea ends, the mythic shore begins."*

It was Merlin's voice, weaving history into destiny. Through the mist, they glimpsed land — Not a port of Europe, but something other. An isle that shimmered like a dream half-remembered. Avalon. And upon its green shores, a company of knights awaited them — Arthur's Round Table, their armour gleaming with the gold of sunrise. Sir Gawain stepped forward first, his voice ringing like steel. "Strangers from distant waters, who dares approach the court of the High King?"

Our order falls beneath the hand of tyrants. Our treasure must not fall with it. We seek sanctuary… and alliance." The gathered knights fell silent. For in their hearts, they felt the turning of something greater than kingdoms. Here were men forged of the same iron — Bound by oath, tempered by faith.

Then Arthur himself emerged from the mist, the Sword Excalibur at his side, and the weight of a crown not of gold, but of destiny. Merlin walked beside him, his eyes alight with secret knowing.

"You have travelled beyond the world of men," Arthur said. "Here, gold is worthless, and crowns hold no power. But courage… courage has a place at my table."

One by one, the Templar knights knelt upon Avalon's soil. And Merlin, with hands both mortal and mystical, drew upon the ground a circle —A new ring of fellowship, joining Templar and Arthurian knights. The Grail's guardians had found their refuge. The Round Table had found its mirror. And a new chapter in legend began.

In the days that followed, the gold they carried was hidden, not in vaults of stone, but in places where no tyrant could reach — Buried in story, wrapped in myth, guarded by silence. And so the world forgot where those ships had landed… But the *whisper* endured.

Where Avalon lies, the treasure remains — not merely of wealth, but of knowledge, power, and a vision of a kingdom that lives beyond time. Dawn crept over Avalon like a golden veil, and the morning mists curled low upon the lake. The Templar banners hung beside Arthur's own, two emblems — one of the cross, the other of the dragon — Stirring in the same wind.

In the Great Hall of the Round Table, A silence fell as Merlin rose. His staff struck the stone floor three times, and the air shimmered with something older than time itself.

"Knights of Arthur. Knights of the Temple. The Grail does not rest in one place — it *calls* to those who are worthy. And now," he said, "its voice has reached Avalon."

He spoke of a hidden path, beyond the mortal realm — a road carved not upon earth, but through the veins of myth itself.
There lay the Grail, vessel of divine mystery, and beside it, the Ark of the Covenant, radiant with the fire of heaven. But such treasures are never unguarded. In the shadow of the Grail, dark powers stirred—those who hungered for gold, power, or eternal life. Merlin named them only once, in a whisper: *"The Brotherhood of the Black Star."*

And so it was decided. Two orders would ride as one. At Arthur's right hand — Sir Gawain, Sir Galahad, and Lancelot, Knights whose courage was sung by bards. At the Templar Master's side —

Hugues de Moray and twelve of his sworn brethren, Warriors forged in the crucible of holy wars.

Through forests older than kings, they rode. Beneath moonlight, they crossed rivers that whispered of forgotten empires. Templar discipline met Arthurian valour, and their bond grew like steel tempered in the forge.

Along the way, Merlin traversed the unseen paths. He conversed with the stars, ravens, and the wind. It was he who first recognised the signs — markings on ancient stones, signs from the Temple of Solomon, pointing towards the Vault of Light.

But the darkness was not resting. Riders in black pursued them. Their cloaks bore no emblem — only the cold hunger for power. The Brotherhood of the Black Star had its sights on the Grail. Thus, the quest became a race, light against shadow, destiny against the long reach of oblivion.

One night, by a fire deep within the whispering wood, Arthur turned to the Templar Master. "You carry a burden of gold," he said, "but your true treasure is your *faith*." The Master nodded slowly. "And you, King Arthur, carry a crown — but your power is your *dream*."

And Merlin, from the shadows, smiled. For this — this union of vision and faith — was what he had long foreseen. Two orders, born in different ages, Woven together to guard a secret too great for any single hand. At dawn, the horns sounded. The quest for the Grail and the Ark had truly begun.

For forty days and forty nights, they rode beneath stars that seemed to burn with purpose. Their path wound through whispering forests, over rivers of silver, and across plains where no mortal map could guide them. At last, the signs Merlin had read in stone and star converged upon a single place: A vast mountain veiled in mist, its peak lost in cloud.

At its foot stood an arch of blackened stone. Carved into its face were the symbols of ages long forgotten, Signs of Solomon, runes of Avalon, and the sacred cross of the Temple. When Merlin's staff touched the earth, the air trembled. The mountain opened like a book… revealing a cavern bathed in a faint golden glow.

"This," Merlin whispered, "is the Vault of Light. Within lies what kings crave and tyrants fear — the Grail… and the Ark of the Covenant."

All were gathered — Arthur, Lancelot and Gawain side by side, Galahad in his simple white mantle, Kay with arms folded tight, Bedivere listening like a hound at a hunt. Even the younger knights, their eyes bright with faith, leaned forward to catch each word.

Merlin lifted his staff. Then all fell utterly silent.

"And let us speak now of the Grail," Merlin began, his voice like wind through ancient stones, "for it is no mere cup, no relic of mortal hands. It is the vessel of the Living Word." The flames trembled as though the very air bent to listen.

"Long ago, in an upper room in Jerusalem, the Lord Jesus sat with those whom He loved most. Before Him lay the bread and the wine. And He said, *When you eat this bread and drink this wine, do so in remembrance of Me. For this is My body, and this is My blood which shall be shed for the forgiveness of sins. For I am the Lamb of God who shall die and rise again so that all may live. "*

The knights bowed their heads. Some made the sign of the cross. Others, though less devout, felt the weight of the words.

"And it was in that moment," Merlin said, raising his hand toward the rafters, "that the simple earthen cup He held — a clay vessel from a humble table — shone with the brightness of heaven. To mortal eyes, it remained but a cup. But to those with faith, it blazed like soft light seemed to move, whether from the fire or some other source, no man could tell.

Lancelot's hand drifted unconsciously to the hilt of his sword, as if a quest had already begun. Galahad's eyes burned with quiet fervour.

Merlin's voice deepened: "But the Grail is not alone. Long before Christ walked among men, the Ark of the Covenant was fashioned at God's command. Within its golden walls rests the stone of Law —the Ten Commandments Moses brought down from the mountain. Upon these words were carved the path by which men must walk if they are to live in harmony with the Divine."

The knights listened as though the very stones surrounding them leaned closer. "There, too, lies the staff of Moses. With it, he parted the waters of the sea so that his people might walk to freedom. He struck the rock, and water flowed for the thirsty. And before the court of Pharaoh, that same rod turned to a serpent to shake the pride of a tyrant and loosen the chains of the chosen."

Arthur leaned forward, his crown catching the firelight like a star.

"The Grail," Merlin said, his voice soft now, "is the cup of promise — the sign of the New Covenant. The Ark is the chest of the Old Law and the staff of deliverance. One is flesh, one is stone. One is the Word made living, one the Word carved in fire. Together, they are the pillars of our faith, the twin beacons of heaven and earth." Somewhere far off, the night owl called — a lonely sound beneath the dark heavens.

"And mark me well," Merlin said, lifting his staff high, "there will come a day when men shall seek these relics not for faith but for power. Kings will march, empires will burn, blood will stain the ground in the name of the Grail and the Ark.. But the Grail will not be found by iron or by crown. It will reveal itself only to the pure heart. The Ark will not be broken open by force — it will rest where the Lord wills."

He turned then to Arthur, and for a heartbeat, the wizard seemed taller than any man, a shadow wrapped in light. "And so," Merlin declared, "let the knights who sit here not only bear swords of steel, but hearts sharpened by faith. The great quests that lie ahead are not won on battlefields alone. They are won in the secret chambers of the soul."

The fellowship entered as one—Arthur at the head, Hugues de Moray at his side, their knights close behind. Inside, the air was warm, alive with the hum of something ancient — A power neither wholly divine nor mortal. The walls shimmered with light that had no source. Golden mosaics told stories of a covenant between heaven and earth. And at the heart of that cavern stood two relics on a single stone altar: the Grail, radiant with living light, and the Ark, veiled in linen, glowing like dawn behind a storm. For a breathless moment, all knelt in silence. But silence does not last long in the shadows when shadows walk. From the dark mouth of the cavern, the Brotherhood of the Black Star emerged. Cloaked in black, their eyes like coals, they moved with the precision of a serpent. Their leader stepped forward, silver mask gleaming. "The Grail is not for kings," he hissed. "Nor knights. It belongs to no one… and to whoever can *take it*."

Steel rang against stone as swords left their scabbards. The battle for the Grail had begun. The cavern erupted in light and fury. Gawain and Galahad clashed with black riders beneath the altar's glow. Lancelot's blade sang against dark steel. The Templars, their white mantles streaked with blood and dust, formed a living wall around the Ark.

The knights rose as one, as if some old vow had been renewed. Their swords glimmered in the golden light. And in that moment, beneath the weight of Merlin's prophecy, the Quest of the Grail was born.

As the battle raged, Arthur and Hugues de Moray fought side by side. Their blades moved as one, a dragon and a cross entwined. And slowly, the Brotherhood faltered. For though their numbers were significant, they had no unity. Greed is a poor shield.

Then the leader of the Brotherhood lunged for the Grail. But Galahad — pure of heart — stepped forward. He did not strike with his sword. He knelt, lowering his weapon. And the Grail itself flared with blinding light. A wind like the breath of creation swept through the Vault. The Brotherhood screamed as their shadows were unmade. The mountain trembled. The darkness fled. When silence returned, the fellowship stood together — bloodied but unbroken. The Grail pulsed softly, as if acknowledging their bond.

The Ark gleamed like a hidden sun. Merlin leaned on his staff, his eyes glimmering with quiet knowing. "The Grail does not belong to us," he said. "It belongs to the ages. And the ages will keep its secret through those who carry its story."

Arthur placed a hand upon the Templar Master's shoulder. "Then we will be its guardians," he said. "Not for power. Not for glory. But to keep the flame alive."And so the Vault of Light was sealed again — Not by stone, but by silence. Only those bound by oath and destiny would ever find it again. Outside, the sun rose over Avalon like a promise. The sun rose upon Avalon like a crown of gold, its light spilling across the lake as though heaven itself had opened its hand. The fellowship returned from the Vault of Light not as they had left. Their swords bore the dust of battle. Their eyes held the weight of what they had seen. And their hearts carried something far greater than gold: a secret.

Merlin walked at the front of the company, his robe brushed by the morning mist. Behind him came Arthur, crowned by dawn,
and beside Arthur rode Hugues de Moray, Master of the Temple, his mantle still marked with the red of sacrifice.

The Grail and the Ark were carried with reverence, wrapped in white and gold, their light seeping through the cloth like starlight through silk. Avalon awaited them in silence. The lake mirrored Merlin, who raised his staff high. The lake stirred. The air thickened. The mists of Avalon gathered, curling like living veils around the relics.

With a gesture, Merlin summoned a circle of fire and water, and the Grail and the Ark rose upon a column of light, hovering above the lake like a star returning to the heavens. Then, slowly, they sank beneath the waters, into a chamber not built by hands, where no sword nor crown could ever reach.

Then night had descended upon Camelot, drawing a shroud of silver mist across the land. The last echoes of the Great Hall faded into the distance, and Merlin walked alone beneath the arching boughs of the ancient forest — his forest — where no crown or sword dared command.

The trees here were as old as the memory of the earth. Their branches leaned together as if whispering secrets of the age before kings. Beneath their canopy, Merlin cast off his cloak and let the night wind touch the face that men seldom saw unshadowed.

He walked until the moss grew thick beneath his feet, until the air smelled of rain and root. There, at the foot of an oak older than the oldest tale, Merlin sank to the earth and let his staff rest across his knees.

"Here," he murmured, "here I was formed."

Once upon a Time.

The wizard closed his eyes. Memory stirred like smoke in the dark.

He saw again the dim light of that night long ago, when a mortal woman — his mother — cried out in a chamber of stone, and an unseen hand moved through the air. His father was not of this world. A spirit of the Otherworld had passed into the mortal plane, its seed falling like a spark into human clay. "Half of earth," Merlin whispered, "half of shadow. A foot in both worlds... and belonging fully to neither."

The wind rustled the leaves above him. The forest, which had always known his heart, answered in soft sighs.

He remembered his youth, when voices came to him unbidden — the whispers of stars, the counsel of stones, the laughter of streams. He had understood too much, too soon. The world of men had both feared and needed him. And so he had become what no one else could be: a bridge between two worlds brought to life through the pen of storytellers.

And so, Merlin closed his eyes beneath the oak and let his mind drift down through the roots of the earth, backward through time — past the Round Table, past the stone and the sword, past kings and pilgrims — back to the womb where the two worlds met.

The wind rose, and in it came the faintest laughter — neither angel nor demon, but something older. The forest remembered. And Merlin, the bridge between realms, remembered too.

So, through the eyes of Merlin, the great wizard, we relive King Arthur, a legendary figure in British folklore, often regarded as a noble king and valiant warrior, central to Celtic mythology. His stories, originating from the fifth century CE, emphasise themes of chivalry, honour, and national unity, with Camelot being the famed court where he and his knights gathered. Arthur is known for his emblematic sword, Excalibur, bestowed upon him by the Lady of the Lake, and his association with the wise wizard Merlin. The tales depict Arthur's extraordinary adventures, including his establishment of the Round Table, a symbol of equality among his knights, nd his quest for the Holy Grail, a revered Christian relic. His life is marked by his marriage to Guinevere and by the betrayal of his knight, Lancelot, which foreshadows the eventual downfall of his reign. The author, to colour the myth, includes the Ark of the Covenant as a symbolic reference to both Christian and ancient biblical texts, thereby enhancing the story's context.

The mythology surrounding Arthur suggests historical roots in the struggles of early Britain against invaders, with references to him appearing in medieval literature, notably Geoffrey of Monmouth's writings and Sir Thomas Malory's *Le Morte d'Arthur* —while there are references to other authors of later vintage in the tale that follows—are related in the manner of many stories that Monmouth wrote centred around kings, princes and knights, all, of which were central to his Arthurian mythology, it is in drawing upon those with that style, this story will unfold similarly.

So let's begin again…

It was many years after Merlin withdrew from the world of men that the forest became his sanctuary once more. The wars of kings had raged on — kingdoms rose and fell like waves breaking on a forgotten shore. Empires and petty fiefdoms, blood feuds and border wars, all spun on like a wheel without end. But in the green silence beneath the old oaks, Merlin listened not to the clash of swords but to the whispers of spirits.

In those shadowed glades, the wild enchantments came back to him. The breath of the Otherworld curled around the trunks of trees like mist, and the night winds carried voices no mortal ear could hear. Here, the wizard once again became Merlin the Enchanter, not the king's counsellor, not the prophet of Camelot, but the child of two worlds — spirit and flesh intertwined. And in that stillness, a thought took root. "What the sword could not unite," he murmured, "a story may yet bind."

For centuries, the land had been soaked with the blood of men who could not live under a single king. The dream of peace had broken like a mirror beneath the weight of ambition. Yet Merlin, who had seen empires rise and fall, knew that legends outlive kings—steel rusts. Crowns fade. But myths endure.

He sat beneath the great oak on a mist-drenched morning, his staff across his knees, his hair stirred by the forest's breath—the still air. He began to shape a story—not of the kings that were, but of the king that should be. A tale of Camelot: a place not bound to any one hill or fortress, but a beacon of unity, honour, and light. A Round Table, where no man sat above another. A vision, not a fact. "Let them not fight for thrones," he whispered, "but for an idea."

So once more, Merlin returned to the mind of Gregory of Monmouth, where he had already implanted the idea of King Arthur, a boy who would be king, but he had not expanded upon the idea until he had thought it through.

So back in the cloisters and study halls of learning, the man who loved to research the past was Gregory of Monmouth, scholar, scribe, and keeper of half-remembered histories. His ink-stained hands worked tirelessly to give shape to the tangled memory of Britain's kings. He traced old chronicles, heard tales from wandering bards, and pieced together the shattered fragments of the island's past. And it was into this man's dreaming mind that Merlin sent the next seed. Not in the form of speech. Not in ink. But in the whispering way of spirits. Through the thin veil between sleeping and waking, Merlin's thought became Gregory's inspiration. Like mist seeping beneath a door, it entered softly, without resistance.

Gregory dreamed of a golden hall by a river. Of a king whose sword gleamed in the sunlight. Of knights whose honour was their bond. Of a queen whose beauty lit the court like dawn. And at the heart of it all —Merlin himself, a shadow in the torchlight, guiding from the edges. Soon, ink met parchment as Merlin unfolded the dream of his making into the keen mind of the writer.

And so Merlin, sitting beneath the twisted boughs of an ancient oak, spoke softly into the night as though he were recounting the tale to the very spirits who once shared his company.

"There was a time," he began, "when Britain groaned beneath the weight of war and the folly of kings. And there rose among them one Uther Pendragon — a man of great strength, a warrior of noble blood, yet one who could not master the tides of his own heart. He ruled by the sword more than by wisdom, and though the realm bowed to his crown, his passions often overran his reason."

Uther had long been consumed by a hunger that no victory could quench — the love of Igraine, the fair and noble wife of Gorlois, Duke of Cornwall. Igraine was known for her grace and virtue, and it was said that when she entered a hall, even the music stilled to watch her pass.

But Uther's desire was not tempered by restraint. He was a king who, in his bloodline, carried whispers of the Otherworld — restless spirits that stirred his darker impulses. When his longing for Igraine grew unbearable, he sought out the counsel of the one man who walked between mortal and spirit realms: Merlin.

The wild man of the forest received him not as a king but as a wayward soul. Beneath the shroud of mist and oak leaves, Uther pleaded for the power to claim the woman he loved. Merlin, his eyes deep with the knowledge of both mortal frailty and divine consequence, spoke but one condition:

"You shall have one night only, Uther Pendragon," Merlin said, his voice like the rustling of wind through old branches. "And when a child is born of this union, the babe shall be mine to guard. The magic of this will occur, I swear to the stars and stones. And this you shall not break. For I have put into the mind of the one who dreams of this child, a scribe who will tell more of this tale. "

Desire clouded Uther's judgment, and he agreed without hesitation. That night, beneath a sky silvered by a pale moon, Merlin wove his enchantment. He cloaked Uther in the very likeness of Gorlois — his voice, his face, his every gesture. In this guise,

Uther entered Tintagel Castle, and Igraine, believing her husband returned from war, received him into her chamber.

And so Arthur was conceived — not in truth but in deception, in the tangled crossing of mortal desire and sorcery's will. As the tide of fate would have it, Gorlois fell in battle that same night. When Igraine learned the truth, she was torn between grief and a strange, solemn understanding.

Merlin came to claim the child, as was promised. And though the court whispered, none dared challenge the enchanter's will. He took the babe into the mists, vowing to raise him not as a prince of privilege but as one who would be tempered by trial, forged like steel in the fires of destiny.

"Thus was Arthur born," Merlin murmured to the silent forest, "a child of both love and deception, mortal blood and otherworldly design. And it was I who set the first stone upon the throne, though I knew even then that no great kingdom is built without the shadows that lie beneath its light."

The night deepened. The wind carried the last of Merlin's words into the unseen realms, where memory and myth entwined like roots beneath the earth.

And so it was, in the turning of seasons and the passing of kings, that Uther Pendragon met his end. The great warrior-king fell not to sword or spear, but to the slow undoing of a heart that had burned too fiercely with desire and ambition. With his death came a kingdom without an apparent heir, for Arthur — his true-born son had been raised far from the throne, hidden from those who might have sought to use or destroy him.

Merlin had seen it all before it unfolded — for he knew the ways of both men and fate. He had placed Arthur as an infant in the care of Sir Ector, a loyal knight of quiet honour, where the boy would grow not as a prince but as a humble squire. The boy was raised in a household of a Knight of the realm, who was neither rich nor poor, nor did he seek a higher status, but to serve as a knight to the order of the king. And true to his arrangement with Merlin, Sir Ector took Arthur to be with his mentor, Meltin, who taught him throughout his boyhood the secrets of magic, spells, and sorcery, not for evil but for good.

And so it was, on a night when the moon lay like a silver coin upon the dark sky, that Merlin took Arthur once more into the quiet heart of the forest where the ancient spirits were still said to whisper to those who dared to listen. The stars above shone like watchful eyes, and the earth below hummed with a living stillness.

For Arthur had come the time to discuss a dream he had of himself as a King in charge of a great kingdom, where he would rule many but be troubled by the crown he wore, the duties that bound him, and the walls that engulfed him. "Sit," Merlin commanded softly. "And breathe not as a king, but as a child of the world. Let the crown fall from your thoughts. Let the walls you carry dissolve." Arthur closed his eyes, letting the forest seep into his skin. The scent of pine and damp earth filled his lungs. A faint warmth began to rise from the ground, as if the roots themselves were lending him their strength. Merlin circled him slowly, staff in hand, murmuring words older than any kingdom, words of wind and leaf and star.

Then something wondrous happened. Arthur felt his body grow light, as though the heaviness of command had slipped away like a cloak. The forest floor fell from beneath him, and he found himself hovering—just a hand's span at first—above the ground. His heart raced, but Merlin's calm voice steadied him.

"Rise, Wort," said the old enchanter. "Let the wind be your ally. Trust the sky."

Up he soared, into the cool, clean air, where the land spread out like a painted map beneath him. He swooped and turned like a hawk, tasting the joy of flight. The sea glimmered on the far horizon, mountains rose like sleeping giants, and rivers coiled like silver threads. "What do you see now?" came Merlin's voice from far below.

Arthur laughed—a free, unguarded sound he had not made in years. "I see everything, Merlin—the sea, the mountains, the valleys, the rivers. The land as a whole. But..." He looked down again. "I see no fences. No boundaries."

Merlin's voice rose like the wind itself: "Remember this, Wort. The walls you build are of your own making. They are not on earth. They are not in the sky. They live only in the minds of men. A true king sees beyond them."

And as Arthur floated there, high above the kingdom that would one day be remembered as Camelot, he understood what Merlin had long tried to teach him:

In the dark corners of Britain's fractured realm, barons and lords sharpened their ambitions like blades, each laying claim to the throne of the fallen king. To bring order to the chaos, Merlin wove a test not of blood but of destiny. Upon a cold winter morning, a great stone appeared in the courtyard of the cathedral in London.

And driven deep into that stone was a sword — gleaming though no smith's hammer had touched it in living memory. Upon its blade were inscribed these words:

"Whoso pulleth out this sword of this stone and anvil is rightwise King born of all England."

And so the mighty came — earls, dukes, knights, and princes — each proud, each sure that their strength and bloodline made them the rightful ruler. One by one they tried, and one by one they failed. The sword would not yield.

Merlin, watching from the shadow of the cloisters, waited not for the strong but for the one whom destiny itself would guide. Then came young Arthur — no royal mantle on his shoulders, no crown upon his brow. He came not as a claimant to the throne but as a boy sent on an errand to fetch a sword for his foster-father,

And so it came to pass that on a cold dawn, veiled in mist and prophecy, the people gathered about the great anvil in the heart of Londonium. Upon that anvil lay a sword unlike any other—not the true Excalibur, but a blade forged by Merlin's own apprentice, wrought to Merlin's sacred design. Its steel was bright but not immortal, its song clear but not eternal, for Merlin had woven into it not the everlasting fire of heaven, but a measured enchantment, enough to crown a king but not to sustain an age. Only one hand was destined to draw it easily—Arthur's—and by that act, destiny itself would bend.

Arthur stepped from the shadows and, with both hands, took the sword from the Anvil's grip. As soon as he touched it, the mists around Avalo lit up with a blaze of light and a host of unseen voices — maybe angels — whispered blessings on his reign. The crowd held their breath in tense silence as young Arthur, humble and unassuming, moved forward. Many princes and noble lords had tugged at the blade and failed, each leaving only the clang of frustration behind. But when Arthur laid his hand on the hilt, the sword responded like a loyal dog to its master. A gentle glow spilled from the steel as the blade lifted from the anvil without resistance, like a whisper escaping from prophecy. In that moment, every man and woman there — whether knight, destined for the Round Table, noble of high blood, or pauper in ragged cloth — fell to their knees in reverence.

" Behold the boy king," some murmured." Not of might alone, but of destiny."

The sword was known in that hour as Caledor, the *Kingmaker's Blade*. It carried within it a double power: First, that none but the chosen hand might draw it. Second, that all who gazed upon Arthur with Caledor in his grasp would bow, their hearts compelled by the will of heaven, acknowledging him as their rightful sovereign.
But Caledor was not made to last forever. Merlin, in his hidden wisdom, had forged it with a fading enchantment. Its edge would sing in Arthur's early battles, strike the proud, and carve the name of every man and woman present —be they knights, nobles, princes, or paupers— the legend of Camelot would be instilled into the chronicles of man. Yet Merlin also foresaw the day it would grow dull, the light fading from its core. And at that very hour, another sword would rise—the actual sword of kingship: Excalibur.

Camelot.

Excalibur was no work of mortal hands, but of divine commission. For beyond the mists of Avalon, Archangel Michael had guided its making—a blade once lifted in the celestial war, when Lucifer and his host were cast down from heaven. The archangel's own hand had wielded that fire, and from the echo of that flame the Lady of the Lake would one day offer the sword to Arthur, not as a gift, but as a covenant. "This blade," Merlin whispered to the silent stars, "is but the herald. The true sword sleeps beneath the waters, awaiting the king it shall never betray."

And so Arthur rode out with Caledor at his side from the slender of Camelot, a king anointed not by crown, but by the will of the blade. His knights followed. His enemies trembled. And the legend of the boy who drew the sword from the stone took root, growing like an oak across the ages, whispering still in every age where hope seems lost and heroes are needed.

Merlin's scribe, Gregory of Monmouth, dreamed names where there had been none—stories that would become history; history that would become legend. Names took form, Arthur. Guinevere. Lancelot. Gawain. Excalibur. Avalon. The Round Table. Gregory of Monmouth set down the tale that would outlive all the warring kings who had torn the land apart. A mythology implanted by Merlin, shaped by a scribe's hand, and carried by a thousand tongues to the farthest edges of Christendom. "Let them believe," Merlin whispered from the forest. "For belief is stronger than steel." The wars raged on, but Arthur's shadow grew larger than any throne. Knights, kings, pilgrims, and dreamers would come to measure themselves against this myth. And though the honest Arthur — if ever there was one — had long turned to dust, the legend lived on, bright and unbroken. Merlin, half in this world and half beyond, listened as the wind carried Gregory's tale across valleys and hills. A faint smile touched the wizard's face. "The sword unites the moment," he said softly. "But the story… unites the centuries."

In the years that followed Arthur's drawing of Caledor from the stone, the kingdom of Camelot rose from a patchwork of warring realms to become a beacon of unity and justice. Upon the crest of a green hill, overlooking the silver waters of the River Usk, Arthur built his great hall and fortress, ringed by white stone walls, soaring towers, and banners that caught the wind like the wings of angels.

A dream of Arthur that was Camelot—a place not only of stone and mortar, but of an ideal. Within its gates, justice reigned above power, and honour rose higher than bloodline. Merchants and minstrels, knights and common folk mingled in its courtyards, knowing they walked in the shadow of a king unlike any other.

Caledor—the *Kingmaker's Blade*—became Arthur's weapon of defence, his trusted companion through the early storms of his reign. Though not eternal like Excalibur, it sang when drawn, its voice carrying across the fields like a silver trumpet.

With this blade, Arthur repelled the northern raiders who sought to break the fragile unity of Britain. He drove back the Saxons who crept like shadows along the eastern shores. He fought brigands, petty kings, and usurpers who could not accept the rule of a young man risen from obscurity.

In every battle, Caledor flashed like a shard of dawn, and the men who marched behind Arthur believed they followed more than a king—they followed a destiny. "With each swing of that blade," Merlin later said, "the boy grew into the king, and the legend took root in the soil of Albion."

When the wars of unification were won, Arthur turned not to conquest, but to order and vision. Within the Great Hall of Camelot, he set a vast round table, fashioned of oak from the ancient groves of Avalon. The table had no head and no foot. There was no place of higher or lower rank. At this table sat the Knights of the Round Table—Gawain, Percival, Lancelot, Bedivere, Tristan and many more—each bound by oath to uphold chivalry, truth, and justice.

Every knight's voice carried equal weight in matters of the realm. Laws were spoken openly. Councils were shared. Deeds were judged by their virtue, not their bloodline. It was said: "At Camelot, the king sits among men, not above them."

This governance became a model of unity rarely seen before or since—an age of light amid centuries of darkness.

In the fourth year of Arthur's reign, word spread of a noble maiden from the western lands of Cameliard—Guinevere, daughter of King Leodegrance. She was said to have hair like woven sunlight, eyes like the calm of summer fields, and a mind both keen and kind. Her father, a loyal ally, sent her to Camelot under the banner of peace and friendship.

When Arthur first saw Guinevere riding through the gates of the castle, the tumult of his heart was stilled. Though he had faced enemies without fear, he was struck silent in that moment. Guinevere, for her part, saw not the conqueror nor the king, but the man who bore a destiny with quiet strength.

Their courtship was gentle but sure, like two rivers winding toward the same sea. Guinevere would walk the gardens with him in the twilight, where the walls of Camelot blushed in the sunset. She spoke of peace, while he spoke of duty, and in their words they found a shared dream of what the realm could become.

The court rejoiced at their union. The bells of Camelot rang for seven days and seven nights. Their wedding marked the golden springtime of Arthur's reign, when laughter filled the halls and the Round Table shone with purpose. In those years, Camelot flourished: Roads were made safe for travellers and merchants. Justice was swift, fair, and above corruption. Knights rode on quests not for greed, but for honour. Festivals and feasts filled the calendar with joy and song.

Arthur would ride at dawn with Caledor at his hip, not as a tyrant, but as a guardian of the dream. His knights felt honoured to serve, for they were part of something greater than themselves—a fellowship that stretched from hearth to throne.

And in the evenings, as the sun bled gold across the horizon, Guinevere would stand at the balcony, watching her king return from the fields. Happiness reigned, not as mere mirth, but as a shared spirit that bound the kingdom together. But Merlin, in his quiet watch, knew all enchantments have their hourglass. Caledor's edge was wearing thin. A greater sword, a greater destiny, and greater trials still lie ahead.

And so it was that even as King of Camelot—when the banners of his house flew proud above the ramparts and the songs of his knights echoed through the great hall—Arthur would still find himself drawn back to the deep green silence of the forest. It was there, away from courtiers and the noise of governance, that he returned to Merlin—not as a king, but as the boy once called Wort.

The forest had not changed. The same moss clung to the stones, the same river murmured its old secrets, and the same ancient oaks stood like sentinels of forgotten time. Here, Arthur could lay down the weight of crown and sword and be simply a seeker again.

"Merlin, my guide," Arthur said one soft twilight, his cloak heavy with the scent of horse and hearth smoke. "There are fences I cannot see but feel all around me—walls of duty, walls of doubt. My knights counsel me in matters of war and court, but not in the strange questions that trouble a man's soul. I am hemmed in by the burden of being king, and the world seems narrower now than when I was a boy."

Merlin, seated upon an old root twisted like a throne of the earth itself, gave a quiet, knowing smile. The years had added to Arthur's stature but had not changed the look in his eyes—the same restless wonder lived there still.

"Ah, Wort," said Merlin, for he alone still called him by that name. "You are like the herb that grows beneath the oak—rooted, but ever reaching toward the light. The walls you speak of are not made of stone. They are the product of your own mind. Power creates its own prisons, and kings are not free just because they wear a crown."

Arthur frowned, gazing down at the forest floor where the first stars of the night blinked through gaps in the canopy. "And how does a king step beyond those walls?"

Merlin rose slowly, leaning on his staff. The breeze stirred his robes, and the scent of pine and earth filled the air.

"By remembering," the old wizard said, "that the world is not only made of laws and duties. The language of the stars still speaks. The rivers still remember your name. Come—sit, listen. The forest has counsel for those who have the patience to hear it."

"To lead men," Merlin whispered, "you must first walk freely within yourself. The crown is not your master, Wort. It is your burden to carry with grace, not with chains."

When Arthur opened his eyes, the stars had brightened, and the night seemed vast again. For a moment, the fences had faded, and he was once more the boy who learned from the wind and the trees. And so it became his quiet ritual—whenever the crown grew too heavy, Arthur would return to Merlin and the forest, to sit in the garden where kingship fell away, and wisdom whispered like wind through leaves.

So they sat together in the garden of the forest—king and mage, as they had in the days of his youth. Merlin bade him close his eyes, to breathe as the trees breathe, to let the noise of Camelot fall away like leaves in autumn. And in that stillness, Arthur found what no council chamber could offer: a clarity born of silence. And from that day forth, Merlin came to live at Camelot to continue as a mentor to King Arthur, providing solace in times of trouble when a united kingdom would turn into a house divided.

And so it came to pass that the golden age of Camelot ripened like wheat beneath the summer sun. The kingdom was prosperous, its knights noble, and its king beloved. Yet beneath the bright surface of those halcyon days, destiny stirred, for no enchantment born of mortal hands can endure forever.

Caledor — the *Kingmaker's Blade* — had sung through a hundred battles and crowned Arthur's early reign with victory. But as the years passed, its song began to wane. The once-radiant steel grew dull; hairline cracks webbed its surface like frost on glass. In the last of Arthur's early campaigns, when northern warbands tested Camelot's borders, Caledor struck an enemy shield and splintered with a sharp, ringing cry that echoed like a bell tolling for the end of an era.

The men who had fought behind that blade lowered their banners in silence. Arthur, holding the broken sword, felt not defeat but the weight of an old prophecy: *"When the herald falls silent, the true sword shall rise."*

Merlin, who had long walked the edges of time, came to Arthur that night in the great hall. The hearth-fire danced like whispering spirits.

"My king," Merlin said, "the blade that made you king was never meant to bear your reign. It was a bridge, nothing more. Now the time has come to claim what was forged beyond the hand of man."

Arthur bowed his head, not in sorrow, but in understanding. For this too was part of the path laid out for him since the day his fingers first touched Caledor's hilt.

Led by Merlin, Arthur rode through mists and forests to the hidden lake of Avalon, where the waters lie still as silver mirrors. The air grew heavy, as though the world itself held its breath. Upon the surface of the lake, a light broke through the fog—a shimmering hand rose, pale as moonlight, and in its grasp was a sword unlike any other.

The blade glowed with a celestial brilliance, its steel forged not in mortal fires but in the white flames of Heaven, guided by the archangel Michael himself. Legends whispered that this was the very firebrand with which Michael drove Lucifer from the gates of Paradise, now remade for a mortal king.

The Lady of the Lake emerged, cloaked in mist, her voice like the current beneath the still water. "Take this blade, Arthur Pendragon. It is not a weapon of ambition, but a covenant between the realms of man and the realm of the divine. Wield it with justice, and your kingdom shall be as unyielding as the sword you hold."

He named the sword Excalibur. Unlike Caledor, this blade did not sing of battle — it resonated with truth. It was flawless, ageless, and unbreakable, its edge like the line between day and night. Its hilt gleamed with golden runes no mortal tongue could thoroughly read, for they were written in the language of the stars.

When Arthur returned to Camelot bearing Excalibur, his knights gathered before the gates. The sword shone like a second sun, and its light fell equally upon pauper and prince. It was said that even the fierest hearts felt their pride soften in reverence at its sight.

"This," Merlin proclaimed to the court, "is the Sword of Kings. Not made to conquer, but to keep the peace. To defend, not to rule."

The broken Caledor was laid to rest beneath the foundations of Camelot, buried like the old skin of a serpent shed for something greater. With Excalibur at his side, Arthur's rule entered its high summer. No enemy could best the blade. Kingdoms that once defied him bent willingly to the justice he upheld. Raiders laid down their arms. Distant chieftains sent envoys, not armies. The sword itself seemed to radiate an unspoken law that even the wicked could not ignore.

Under Guinevere's grace and Arthur's hand, Camelot's banners spread across the land like a canopy of gold. The Round Table grew in legend, knights took oaths of chivalry, and quests of honour filled the chronicles: to protect the weak, to uphold justice, to seek the Grail.

But as Merlin watched from the shadows of the great hall, his eyes grew thoughtful. For every golden age is but a sunrise, and the sun must set, even on Camelot.

It was during an age when kingdoms were built through both sword and spirit that Arthur, son of Uther Pendragon, rose from obscurity to the throne of Britain. By the divine guidance of Merlin, prophet and mage of the ancient ways, he had pulled Excalibur from its resting place—an act not driven by might, but by grace. The blade shone with an otherworldly radiance, and it was said that in battle, its edge sang like tempered flame, while in peace, its reflection soothed the hearts of men.

Merlin, who saw beyond the veil of time, proclaimed that this was no standard weapon of war. "It is the covenant between heaven and earth," he told the young king. "For whosoever wields Excalibur must serve both realms — not as conqueror, but as keeper of the sacred balance."

Under its light, Arthur's banner prevailed across the fields of Albion. The Saxon lords bent their knees, and the realm, long divided by greed and vengeance, was brought to harmony. In those days, Arthur fought as one who knew his cause to be just, but he ruled as one guided by faith.

When peace had come, Merlin led the king to a chapel built of white stone near the waters of Avalon. There, on the morning of his Holy Communion, Arthur knelt before the altar. As he bowed his head, a chalice of gold rose from the sacred table, borne aloft by unseen hands. A shaft of light descended from the heavens, and the cup shone brighter than the sun, casting its reflection upon Arthur's brow.

Merlin beheld this wonder and whispered, "Behold, the sign of the Grail — heaven's promise that purity of heart shall reveal divine mystery." From that day forth, Arthur's soul was bound to the quest of the Holy Grail, a mission not of conquest, but of redemption.

Yet the wizard's vision reached even farther. He spoke of another relic — the Ark of the Covenant, hidden since the days when Solomon's temple fell to ruin. "If the Grail is the cup of divine mercy," said Merlin, "then the Ark is the throne of divine law. Together they complete the circle of heaven's covenant."

Arthur, moved by both prophecy and faith, vowed to seek both relics — the Grail of Christ and the Ark of God — and to guard them in a sanctuary beyond reach of evil. In secret counsel with his knights, he declared: "We shall build a hidden palace where faith and wisdom may dwell unseen — a refuge for all ages when the shadow falls again upon the world."

Thus began the twin quests — the pursuit of grace and of power, the joining of Christian revelation with the mysteries of the ancients. And as the years turned, men whispered that within Camelot's heart, Merlin had already begun to weave that sanctuary, unseen by mortal eyes.

When the light of the Grail still lingered in his dreams, Arthur gathered his most valiant companions to his side — men not only of courage but of conscience. Thus was born the Round Table, symbol of equality and divine order.

Merlin, standing before them with the star of Avalon upon his brow, spoke: "No man shall sit above another, for in the eyes of Heaven, kings and knights are but servants of the same light. Herein lies your test — not to rule the world, but to redeem it."

At the Round Table sat the twelve foremost knights, mirroring the apostles of Christ. Each swore to defend the weak, seek the truth, and guard the mysteries of God wherever they may dwell.

It was then that Merlin confided to Arthur the more profound secret: that the Grail and the Ark were twin vessels — one bearing divine grace, the other divine law — and that together, their union would complete the celestial design first revealed to Moses and fulfilled through Christ.

Among Arthur's knights, there were those of special calling — men whose lineage would stretch beyond Albion's shores. Merlin entrusted these chosen few with the Sacred Charge: "When Camelot falls, as all kingdoms must, you shall bear the relics into the world. Across the seas, beyond the deserts, beneath the holy star of the East — guard them until time itself renews the circle."

These knights would one day be known as the Poor Fellow-Soldiers of Christ and the Temple of Solomon — the Knights Templar. Their order, though born of Arthur's table, would endure through ages of faith and fire, carrying the wisdom of Camelot into the Holy Land.

And so it came to pass that when the temple of Jerusalem was uncovered in later ages, significant changes occurred. It was as if the symbols of Arthur's vision were rediscovered: the cross of Christ, the cup of the Grail, and the memory of the Ark's covenant hidden in the east.

Under Merlin's design, Arthur commanded a sanctuary to be raised — not in the open courts of Camelot, but in a hidden vale shrouded by mist. It was said to be half in this world and half in the next, where the air shimmered with the voices of angels. There the Grail was to be kept, awaiting the hour when humanity would again be worthy of its light.

Merlin named this refuge *Caer Sidi*, the "Fortress of the Turning Sky." Within its marble halls stood a chamber of gold — the Chamber of the Covenant — where the Ark and the Grail would one day rest side by side. In that place, Arthur swore an oath before God and his knights: "Should darkness rise again, this sanctuary shall remain inviolate. For in these relics lies the memory of divine truth — that mercy and justice are one."

Peace seldom lasts in the realm of men. Even in Camelot, where justice had reigned and the light of the Grail shone brightest, the shadow of envy began to creep. Merlin had warned Arthur that no earthly kingdom could stand forever; for every light casts a shadow, and every covenant must be tested.

On the eve of Pentecost, Merlin stood upon the tower of Camelot and saw a single star fall from the heavens, burning red as it descended into the west. He turned to Arthur and said, "The light of the Grail wanes, my king. Betrayal is born not from enemies, but from those who love too fiercely." Merlin had long warned of a shadow born not from enemies abroad, but from within Arthur's own bloodline. Among those closest to the throne was Morgana, his half-sister — a sorceress of striking beauty and formidable intellect, once Merlin's own pupil.

In her youth, she had walked the sacred paths of Avalon, where the veil between worlds grew thin and the Grail's light could be glimpsed in a dream. Yet when Merlin forbade her access to the most profound mysteries — those concerning the Holy Grail and the Ark of the Covenant, their guardianship and hidden resting place — her heart, once bright, darkened with resentment.

From envy was born ambition, and from ambition came deceit. Through spell and illusion, she drew Arthur into her enchanted chamber, weaving visions of destiny and desire. The king, overcome by enchantment and unaware of her true intent, was ensnared. From that night was conceived Mordred, the child of shadow — a son of both royal and forbidden blood.

Merlin, visualising the deception of Mordred to come, wept in silence. "The serpent now coils within the crown," he said. "For the sin born of ignorance shall be the sword that sunders Camelot."

As the years went by, Mordred grew more prideful and cunning, his heart torn between love for the father he hardly knew and the dark advice of his mother, Morgana. When the time arrived, he would rise not as heir but as opponent — and the prophecy of Camelot's downfall would come true.

Long before the fields of Camlann were stained with blood, Merlin foresaw Camelot's doom. The signs had gathered like storm clouds over the years — betrayal, pride, and the slow dimming of the Grail's light.

One night, as thunder roared above the citadel, the prophet stood on the battlements, his cloak billowing in the wind. Lightning lit up his face, etched with sorrow deeper than time itself. Arthur came forward, tired from the weight of kingship.

"Speak to me truth, old mate," said the king. "Is there no way this realm might yet be saved?" Merlin looked at him and replied: "The wheel has turned, my king. The circle that began with the sword in the stone must close in fire and shadow.
You have ruled with grace and fought with faith — but your sin was innocence. You trusted where guile was sown.

Merlin, seeing in advance what would come to pass, wept in silence. "The serpent now coils within the crown," he said. "For the sin born of ignorance shall be the sword that sunders Camelot."

Betrayal.

In the stillness before dawn, when even the stars seemed to hold their breath, Merlin beheld a vision of the end. The mists of Avalon parted before his eyes, and he saw a battlefield drenched in crimson light — the plain of Camlann, where destiny itself would be tested. He saw Arthur, noble and weary, bearing the weight of both crown and cross. In the shadow of Mordred, born of sin and sorrow, advancing beneath a banner black as night. And between them, he saw the Grail — its light flickering, dimmed by the folly of men.

Then the voice of prophecy came upon him, as if spoken by the breath of Heaven itself: "When father and son meet in wrath, when the sword forged in holiness is stained with kin's blood, when Avalon weeps and the Grail is hidden from mortal sight — then shall Camelot fall, and the age of wonder pass into legend."

Merlin, trembling, fell to his knees. He knew that no spell, no wisdom, could avert what must be. The will of Heaven was written in fire.

It came to pass that Arthur, returning from the northern wars, found his hall defiled; for he was confronted with a deception that tore at his heart with great sorrow, and his very soul seemed to be pieced too. The knights had assembled in the great hall, and all but Lancelot were present. It was then that Mordred, who had been whispering in the ears of many knights—not just those of the Round Table — put his snare into play to trap Arthur with his desire to bring down the kingdom of Camelot.

Before the clouds of rebellion gathered over Britain, another storm was already forming within the very walls of Camelot — a storm of love, loyalty, and sorrow. Among all his knights, Sir Lancelot du Lac shone brightest. He was the mightiest of warriors and the truest of friends — a man of unmatched courage, whose sword had defended Arthur's realm more times than the chronicles could record. To the king, he was brother, champion, and the living image of the chivalric ideal.

Yet even the noblest heart is not safe from the fire of passion. For in those golden years, when peace reigned and the Grail's light still lingered, Lancelot's eyes fell upon Queen Guinevere, Arthur's beloved wife. At first, their love was silent, veiled in courtesy and restraint, but affection, once kindled, cannot long be contained. In the king's absence during the northern wars, their hearts and fates entwined — a union of beauty and betrayal that would one day undo the kingdom both had sworn to serve. When whispers of the affair reached the court, Mordred, ever watchful and cunning, saw his chance. He recalled a law Arthur himself had written — that no knight nor queen who broke faith or defiled their sacred vows should be spared the judgment of the realm. And so Mordred, feigning loyalty, urged Arthur to uphold the very code that had made Camelot just.

"My lord," he said, "if the law binds all men, then it must also bind the crown. For justice cannot live where mercy favours the guilty." Arthur's heart was torn. He loved his queen beyond reason and his knight beyond measure. Yet he was bound by the oath of his own making — that even kings must yield to the rule of law.

Arthur summoned his Council of the Round Table, and the knights cast their votes. Five, moved by compassion, pleaded for mercy and reconciliation — Arthur among them. But six others, bound by strict honour, declared that the Queen must face the law's decree: to be burned at the stake for her betrayal of the crown.

Thus, the king was caught between love and justice. "I am both ruler and man," he said, "and in this, both are undone." Guinevere was taken to the Tower, her chamber lit by the flickering torches of those who once adored her. The people of Camelot wept in silence, for none doubted her beauty nor her sorrow.

As the fateful day drew near, Lancelot returned, riding hard through the dawn with knights still loyal to him. He stormed the courtyard as the pyre was being raised, his sword flashing like white fire. A fierce battle erupted between Lancelot's company and the royal guard — brother fighting brother beneath the very towers that once sang of peace.

Lancelot reached the Queen and cut her bonds, crying, "Come, my lady — for I would rather burn beside you than live beneath the ashes of your innocence!"

Together they fled into the night, the gates of Camelot closing behind them like the tolling of a bell. The rescue divided the kingdom beyond repair. Arthur's heart broke beneath the weight of love lost and loyalty betrayed. Many knights, once bound by unity, took sides — some to Lancelot's banner, others to Mordred's. And in that hour of sorrow, Merlin foresaw the deeper ruin yet to come — that the wound of love would open the way for the wound of war. He turned to Arthur and whispered, "The heart has been struck, my king. And from this wound, the realm itself shall bleed."

Lightning flashed upon the horizon like the forge of the gods, and thunder rolled as if Heaven itself mourned.

In his tent, Arthur prayed beside Excalibur, the sword that had once crowned him king. "Forgive me, Lord," he whispered, "for my blindness. I sought to rule with love, yet love has undone me. Grant that my fall may not be the end, but the seed of something greater."

Merlin entered silently, bearing the Grail wrapped in a linen cloth. "This shall not be lost," he said. "When all else falls to ruin, the Grail and the Covenant shall endure. You go to death, my king — but your spirit shall sleep beneath the western mists until Britain's need is greatest."

Arthur rose and took his friend's hand. "Then watch for me, Merlin. When I return, may we build anew — not with swords, but with hearts redeemed." Outside, the wind began to howl, and the torches guttered. The earth trembled beneath the tread of gathering armies.

The flame that had once lit Camelot now burned against it.

The escape of Lancelot and Queen Guinevere divided the Round Table, turning friend against friend and shaking the realm's foundation. What began as love became legend, and what began as loyalty became rebellion.

Arthur, broken in spirit, sought neither vengeance nor peace, but truth. Yet truth was the cruellest sword of all. He knew the fault was not Lancelot's alone, nor Guinevere's, but his own — for building a kingdom on mortal hearts, when even kings are subject to weakness.

As the embers of his heart cooled, another fire began to rise — one far darker.

In the king's absence, Mordred moved like a shadow through the court. He spoke softly to the discontented, reminding them that Camelot's laws were broken, its honour defiled. "A kingdom ruled by love," he whispered, "cannot endure. We need strength — a ruler unbent by sentiment." Soon, whispers became oaths. Knights who once feasted beneath Arthur's banner swore allegiance to Mordred, who claimed descent not merely as the king's nephew, but his son, born of blood and betrayal.

With Merlin withdrawn into silence and Lancelot in exile across the sea, Mordred declared himself Regent of Camelot. He sealed the gates, took the crown from its resting place, and proclaimed that the age of Arthur was ended.

When word arrived to Arthur of Mordred's further treachery, he turned to his men and said, "We have fought wars for God and for Britain. Now we must fight one for the soul of both."

And so he gathered his loyal host — those who had not fled to Lancelot's side nor bowed to Mordred's deceit — and began the long march to where the battle to rule or divide would take place.

Merlin appeared to him once more, his staff dimmed, his robes torn by wind and years. "You go now to fulfil the prophecy, my king," he said. "There is no victory ahead, only destiny. For the serpent born of sorrow shall strike the lion, and the lion shall slay the serpent — and in their blood the realm shall be reborn."

Arthur looked upon him, weary yet resolute. "Then let it be done, old friend. Better to fall in truth than to live in deceit."

Lightning flashed upon the horizon like the forge of the gods, and thunder rolled as if Heaven itself mourned.   In his tent, Arthur prayed beside Excalibur, the sword that had once crowned him king. "Forgive me, Lord," he whispered, "for my blindness. I sought to rule with love, yet love has undone me. Grant that my fall may not be the end, but the seed of something greater."

Merlin entered silently, bearing the Grail wrapped in a linen cloth. "This shall not be lost," he said. "When all else falls to ruin, the Grail and the Covenant shall endure. You go to death, my king — but your spirit shall sleep beneath the western mists until Britain's need is greatest."

Arthur rose and took his friend's hand. "Then watch for me, Merlin. When I return, may we build anew — not with swords, but with hearts redeemed."

Outside, the wind began to howl, and the torches guttered. The earth trembled beneath the tread of gathering armies. The storm had come, and a bell of death was sounding its knoll.

Dawn came grey and cold over the field of Camlann, shrouded in mist. Two armies faced each other in uneasy silence — father and son, king and betrayer. Above them, the sky churned with thunderclouds, and the wind carried the scent of rain and blood yet to be spilled.

Arthur rode at the head of his host, Excalibur gleaming faintly in his hand. Across the field, Mordred sat astride a black steed, his armour dark as the storm behind him, his eyes burning with bitter triumph. They might have been reflections of one another — two halves of a broken whole.

Before the battle was joined, Arthur called for a truce. He rode forward alone, save for two trusted knights. Mordred did the same, each wary but compelled by fate.

"Stand down, my son," Arthur said, his voice carrying through the mist.
 "No good can come of this. Camelot is not yours to take — it is the dream of a people, not the spoil of a crown."

Mordred's lip curled.

"Your dream died the day you betrayed your own law. You spoke of justice and love, but broke both. I am what you made me — and I will not kneel."

Arthur bowed his head in sorrow.

"Then may God forgive us both."

High on a ridge overlooking the field of Camplann, where the memorable battle for love of Queen Guineve and the power of a throne would be fought for, stood Merlin. He watches as the knight of the Round Table of King Arthur's court, who once stood in honour of the Sacred Charter of the Round Table of knighthood.

For it was a statement as spoken by King Arthur, and sealed by Merlin of Albion.

In the year when peace first dawned upon our realm,
And the stones of Camelot were set beneath Heaven's gaze,
We gathered — king and knight, priest and sage —
Beneath the light of God, to swear this covenant of honour.

And now not by the truth within the hearts did Knights ride to battle, but in opposing loyalty, in the will of the flesh and in some deception. Had it been regarded as a united Covenant, the battle of knights against knights and brother against brother might not have happened. It

It was in that moment that Merlin wept as he recalled:

"By the will of Heaven and the grace of God, we take up the sword not for conquest, but for truth. Let no man draw blade in pride nor vengeance, but in the defence of the weak, the innocent, and the just."

"Our word shall be our seal. Our deeds shall be our testament. Let no lie pass our lips, nor treachery dwell in our hearts. For the Round Table is the mirror of our souls —and no stain may rest upon it."

"Let the strong remember the frail, and the victor spare the fallen. Strike not without cause, nor take joy in the shedding of blood. For the sword that serves hate shall one day turn upon its master."

"Let no man stand above the law, not even the king who made it. Justice shall be the throne upon which we sit. Each knight shall be the brother of another. Each shall guard the honour of his fellows as his own. Betrayal shall be the death of faith — and faith the life of all."

"Seek ye always the light of the Holy Grail, not for pride nor glory, but that the soul of man may draw nearer to the divine. For the Grail is not a cup of gold — it is the heart made pure." "So long as these vows are kept, Camelot shall never die. Though stone may crumble and time may fade its name, the spirit of the Round Table shall live wherever men act with honour."

Then Merlin recalled, when each Knight had spoken those words, Arthur drew forth Excalibur, and touched the point to the centre of the tab, — whereupon light filled the hall, and the Grail's radiance shone above them like a star.

Each knight rose and placed their right hand upon the table's rim, saying as one voice: "By faith, by honour, and by the light of God, we pledge our lives to the dream of Camelot."

And Merlin, in his deep and ancient voice, whispered: "So it is written. So it shall endure — until the King returns."

Merlin stood alone, his cloak whipping like a banner of mourning. Below him, the two armies waited — Arthur's loyal host to the west, and Mordred's black standard to the east — each line shimmering with the restless breath of men who knew they might not see the dawn.

Merlin's staff trembled in his hand. The magic that once sang in the stones of Britain now lay heavy in his heart. He whispered into the wind: "How did it come to this? A kingdom forged in light, undone by shadows of its own making."

He saw before him not soldiers but ghosts — the faces of men he had once anointed, who had once sworn the sacred oath of the Round Table. Their voices still echoed in his mind: *By faith, by honour, by the light of God, we pledge our lives to the dream of Camelot.* Yet that dream had faltered.

Merlin's eyes turned toward the memory of brighter days — when laughter rang through the halls, when the Grail's light burned pure in the hearts of men. He saw Arthur, noble and devout, whose every breath sought to mirror Heaven's justice. He saw Lancelot, his most faithful friend and bravest knight, loyal beyond measure — yet undone by love.

 And between them, he saw Guinevere, fair and gracious, torn between her duty to the crown and the longing of her heart. "Ah, love," Merlin murmured, "the sweetest of gifts and the cruellest of fates. The sword could not slay Camelot — but love, mislaid, has broken its spine."

Eternal Triangle

He remembered how he had warned Arthur: that the greatest threat to a kingdom of honour was not the enemy beyond its walls, but the fracture of trust within.

And Mordred — the serpent born of sin — had known this truth too well. He whispered lies in the ears of the discontented, fanning jealousy into flame, until faith itself turned to ash.

Merlin lifted his gaze toward the Round Table's knights, now divided across the plain. Brothers who once feasted together now sharpened blades for one another's blood. Their bright banners — Gawain's sun, Bedivere's cross, Bors's lion — fluttered in the wind like dying prayers. "They have forgotten," Merlin said softly, tears streaking his weathered cheeks. "Forgotten the oath that bound them — to truth above pride, to mercy above wrath."

He could almost hear Arthur proclaiming that sacred charter long ago, and the knights repeating it in unison, their hearts pure and resolute. Now those same hearts beat with hatred, and the holy bond was broken. Even the Grail itself, he feared, had hidden its light from men.

Merlin fell to his knees, the earth trembling beneath him.
 His tears darkened the soil where countless would soon fall.
 He struck the ground with his staff, and the wind seemed to answer, carrying his words across the field:

"O Lord of Heaven, forgive them! They sought Your kingdom on earth and found only the weakness of their own flesh.

They built a round table so that none would stand above another — yet pride crept in, and love was twisted by deceit."

He closed his eyes, seeing visions of what was to come — Arthur and Mordred locked in mortal embrace, Lancelot exiled across the sea, Guinevere cloistered in sorrow, and Camelot's towers sinking beneath the weight of its own tragedy.

"This is not the end," Merlin whispered through his tears. "The dream cannot die, only sleep. When the hearts of men remember what it means to be pure, the King shall rise again."

The thunder rolled closer now. Below, the first horns sounded — the call to arms, the herald of doom. Merlin stood, leaning on his staff, and turned his face toward the storm.

A single tear glimmered on his cheek like a fallen star. "So it is written," he said. "So it must be."

And as the armies began their march, the prophet wept — for the king, for the knights, for the dream of Camelot, and for the frailty of the human heart.

Now we must not forget that redemption comes through suffering in the ways of the spirit and man, for in these well-remembered writings of Gregory of Monmouth, he adapted another scroll of interpretation. As a scholar, he may have drawn from the marriage in Greek myth of Zeus and Hera. His unfaithfulness to the marriage vows could have been seen as a moral stance even in his days, for in the mythical world of Zeus, he was condemned for his adultery. For there was a resolution in the marriage of Zeus and Hera, and perhaps there is a resolution to the problem of infidelity, literally or fantastically, in that of King Arthur, Queen Guinevere and Sir Lancelot.

It is a rather unique love triangle in the story of King Arthur, where Queen Guinevere's love for the King's best friend comes into play. In the best of all myths, we learn of the pain of betrayal in more ways than one. It is virtually unique because none of the participants in the love triangle attempts to destroy one another; instead, they find reconciliation and inner peace through integrity, loyalty to friendship, and a recognition of the sacred nature of deep and heartfelt love.

So, forgive me for digressing from the impending battle between the opposing forces of King Arthur, Lancelot, and their love for Guinevere. This conflict is orchestrated by the devilish actions of Mordrid, the illegitimate son and self-proclaimed heir to the throne of Camelot, leading to its downfall. We shall return to the battle and the dreaded ending of that saga later. For now, I am more inclined to share another version of events in the lives of King, his wife, and a friend who were drawn into a love triangle that ended differently than the one that so often appears in mythical stories.

After so many years of wars and battles, where Arthur and his Knights had achieved victory over Saxon hordes, he returned home to rule Camelot in peace. Now, with time on his hands, he began to feel lonely and consulted Merlin, his wise advisor. "The time has come," the king announced, "for me to take a wife." Merlin enquired if Arthur had made a choice, and it seems he had. For he told of a wondrous, beautiful princess called Guinevere, the daughter of King Leodegrance of Camelard, and was inflamed with love even before he had met the lady. He had sighted her in the marketplace from a distance and was already smitten.

Now, Merlin, being a prophet, could foresee that the choice would end in tragedy, and seeing the stars in the eyes of his King, remarked: "If I should advise you that Guinevere is an unfortunate choice for you, would that change your mind?"

" No", replied the King.

Merlin more persistently said: " Well, if I should tell you that Guinevere will be unfaithful to you with your dearest and most trusted friend…" King Arthur would have none of it. " I would not believe."

"Of course you would not." Merlin sadly replied. " Every man who has ever lived holds tight to the belief that, for him alone, the laws of probability are cancelled out for love. Even I, who know beyond doubt that a silly girl will cause my death, will not hesitate if that girl passes by. Therefore, you will marry Guinevere. For you do not want advice but only my agreement."

So, as fate would have it, Lancelot had come into King Arthur's life as his most loyal of knights —brave, honest, and faithful. Arthur then sent Lancelot to bring her from her father's house to the king's court to formalise his engagement to her. On the journey, Merlin's prophecy came to pass, and Lancelot and Guinevere fell in love with each other. But neither would consent to break their promise to the king.

Soon after the wedding, King Arthur was called away from his Camelot throne to attend to business in another province. It was then that the son of King Meleagant, a sworn enemy of King Arthur with a kingdom far away, devised a plan to capture Guinevere. He had laid a trap for Guinevere and abducted her, carrying her off to his faraway castle. There he held her in a moated prison —the only way to enter was via a bridge that was well guarded by Badenmagus knights. No one dared go after Guinevere but Lancelot, who made his way through dangerous mountainous land until he reached a valley where he discovered Guinevere's hiding place. He was alone and hopelessly outnumbered when he began to cross the bridge, but although grievously wounded, he rescued Guinevere after killing King Meleagant.

On return to Camelot, Guinevere took pity on Lancelot and insisted on treating his wounds herself. As he lay healing, they began to embrace, and then, at last, the two consummated their secret love.

When Arthur returns to Camelot, the ever-vigilant Merlin, Arthur's mentor and protector, forgets his wisdom and reports a vision where he sees Queen Guinevere and Lancelot in their lovemaking.

And that is where Mordrid uses his deceptive nature, making others in the court aware of the lover's secret. But Arthur, of much wisdom and experience, refrained from violence or accusation and held his counsel, knowing that both his friend and queen suffered greatly due to their love, and both had struggled against it as best they could. And because he loved them both, he was loath to destroy either of them by publicly exposing their betrayal. So he waited, and although all were made wretched because of the love each bore for one another, he held his pain in silence.

But the knights of the court were angry at the shame the queen and Lancelot had brought to the king, and also saw a chance to grasp power and oust the king's best friend from his side. So they plotted to catch Lancelot and Guinevere together to bring the king proof of the betrayal and make public the queen's misdeeds. Among these knights was Mordred, who was the king's illegitimate son and who secretly sought the throne for himself.

That night, the self-seeking men lay in wait for the lovers and burst into the chamber where they lay. But Lancelot escaped, and the knights took the queen prisoner and brought her before the king with proof of her betrayal. So Arthur was forced to go against his will and publicly accuse her of standing trial. Guinevere was found guilty and sentenced to the fire. But as she was dragged to the stake, Lancelot, who had received news of her fate while he lay in hiding, rode forth to rescue her. The battle was a great one, and many knights were slain before Lancelot carried the queen to his castle called Joyous Gard.

Now Arthur could no longer be forgiving, for Lancelot had killed many of his knights. So the king set off with his army to besiege the castle of Joyous Gard. But Lancelot refused to ride forth from the castle, for he would not do battle with Arthur. And then Arthur and Lancelot spoke to each other, and each remembered the love and loyalty they held for each other, and Lancelot repented and swore to give up the queen's love, so Arthur and Lancelot were reconciled.

Arthur could have taken back the queen, but the other knights would not countenance such a spirit of forgiveness. They demanded vengeance, so Lancelot had to come forth to do battle with these knights, lest he be thought a coward. And a great battle followed. During the battle, Arthur and Lancelot met, and tears welled in the men's eyes. But they could not undo what had been done, and the battle went on around them, although these two had made peace with each other.

Eventually, both sides grew exhausted, and an armistice was declared. Arthur returns to court with Guinevere and offers Lancelot his old seat at the Round Table. However, Mordred, seeing power slipping away, plotted to bring about the downfall of all three. He led a large army against the king, and during the battle, the king was fatally wounded by Mordred's spear. Although Lancelot fought alongside Arthur and killed Mordred, who, in his dying breath, reached out for Arthur, calling "Father." Both men, in their final moments—and even afterwards—lay together and finally embraced in death's grasp. When the fighting was over, Lancelot could not bear his guilt and told the widowed queen that he must leave Camelot forever. So he rode off and entered a monastery, spending his days repenting his misdeeds. The queen, too, could not bear either her guilt or the loss of both men she loved, and she took herself to a nunnery.

Years went by, and one night, Lancelot had a vision telling him to visit the queen. When he reached the nunnery where she spent her days, he was told she had died half an hour earlier, and he faced her corpse. Then Lancelot stopped eating and drinking, and he became sicker and sicker. In the end, he pined away and passed on.

Both Lancelot and Guinevere were placed on the same bier and brought to Lancelot's castle of Joyous Gard. All the surviving knights who had sought their destruction in life came together to honour them in death, for they had expiated their sins, and all knew of their great love for each other and the king. All three were forgiven in death who were not forgiven in life. Thus, this myth ends the love triangle with a shining vision of the nobility of the human heart. It portrays a potential that all of us are capable of but which, sadly, is rarely met in real life. None of the characters in this story finds romantic happiness in the ordinary sense. But more importantly than living happily ever after is the absolute loyalty all three showed towards the deepest demands of their souls, even. However, it cost them everything. None of the characters in this story finds happiness in the usual sense.

If the love between Guinevere and Lancelot was anything less than a love of the soul, neither would have given in to temptation. If Arthur's love for both his friend and queen was anything less than a love of the soul, he would have succumbed to anger and revenge, with everyone's full support. There might be times when such a love enters our lives, and if it does, we can understand why the ancients believed it was a divine visitation, over which human will has no power. Often, simple lust or secretly wanting to punish a partner is masked by declarations of grand passion. But the true nature of such desire is revealed when we are faced with the choices faced by these three mythical figures. We might consider ourselves lucky if such fiery tests do not enter our lives; if they do, great suffering is unavoidable for all three. Yes, if life throws such a challenge at us, it's worth remembering the story of Arthur, Guinevere, and Lancelot, which shows that betrayal can be the deepest way we come to understand ourselves and what we really believe in.

Now you may see this as a milk-and-cookie version of the myth, for it is a happy-ever-after tale in the otherworld. It may well suit you, the reader, if you are of the feminine persuasion, but it's not a fitting ending for the likes of us, blooded males. We are not content for justice to soothe the savage beast that dwells in our hearts; we counter the soul's longing for peace with a head for war.

Merlin and the Lady of the Lake

So it came to pass that even Merlin, the wisest of men and the keeper of all secret arts, was not beyond the reach of mortal frailty. For though he could command the winds, converse with spirits, and read the hidden patterns of destiny, he could not rule his own heart. Merlin — prophet, healer, and architect of Camelot — was a man apart. He was versed in the language of the stars, the whispers of herbs, and the power of transformation. At will, he could become the stooped older man with a sickle in his hand, or the bright-eyed boy who spoke riddles of the dawn.

Sometimes he walked as a beggar among men, unseen and unregarded; sometimes he passed as a shadow, neither flesh nor spirit. Yet for all his wisdom, he guarded his solitude. He had never known a woman's embrace, nor allowed himself to love — perhaps because he feared it, probably because he could not comprehend the mystery of it. But fate, which even prophets must obey, had long prepared his fall.

One day, as Merlin wandered through the green woods near the Lake of Broceliande, he beheld a maiden of surpassing beauty.
Her name was Nyneve, though some called her Vivien, and her eyes were as clear as still water. Merlin felt the pulse of life stir within his old heart, and he knew desire for the first time. To win her favour, he cast his glamour and appeared before her in the form of a radiant youth. He conjured visions to delight her —knights and ladies dancing in golden light, minstrels playing upon lutes of silver, and gardens where the air itself seemed to sing. Nyneve watched, silent and smiling, and in her silence, Merlin mistook admiration for affection.

Day by day, she coaxed from him the secrets of his power. She spoke sweetly, asking how the moon bends the tides, although shadows may be woven into invisibility, how love potions might stir the coldest heart. And Merlin, bewitched not by magic but by longing, taught her all he knew — every spell, every word of binding, every charm of sleep. Yet though he gave her his wisdom, she gave him no comfort. She promised that when his teaching was complete, she would be his — but each day she found a new question, and each night she drifted from his arms like mist. At last, even Merlin's vast sight pierced the veil of his own folly. He saw his end written in her eyes and knew she would use his knowledge to entrap him. And yet — even knowing — he could not resist her.

Before his doom was sealed, Merlin came to King Arthur one final time. The great hall was quiet as he entered, his eyes shadowed with sorrow. "My king," he said, "the hour draws near when you must stand alone. The dream of Camelot fades, and I must pass into the earth." Arthur rose in alarm. "Surely, Merlin, with all your knowledge, you can prevent this fate!" Merlin looked upon him gently, and a single tear fell upon the floor. "It is true," he said, "that I know many things — the names of the stars, the language of the stones, the secrets of life and death. Yet in the battle between knowledge and passion, knowledge never wins." And with those words, he turned and departed, never to return to Camelot again. Some say through the trees, one might still hear him whisper: "Beware the sweetness that blinds the wise, for the heart is the oldest magic of all."

Now it may fit within the realm of your imagination, dear reader, to believe that this was the fate of Merlin, to be locked away in a cave of his own making for all eternity. But for a wise magician like Merlin, I will have none of this. There is always a key to unlock the mystery of captivity. Merlin, you will find that you may have fallen for the most complex of all deceivers' quests to gain the ultimate secrets, the one that can never be reversed. However, given that he built the crystal cave for her with the impression of a one-sided key to the cave in its door, he designed an inner keyhole, where, at the appropriate time and place, he would open it to perform further deeds for the betterment of humanity.

And in the forest of Broceliande, Nyneve led him to a cave of crystal light, and there, by her spell, Merlin's body was bound in eternal sleep. Some say he still lives, sealed within the earth, his voice murmuring through roots and rivers, his spirit waiting for the world to remember wisdom. And sometimes, when the wind sighs, he rests in the cave at various intervals of his long life to reenergise until the call to action returns him home to the world again. Then what of the woman who enticed Merlin to reveal all his secrets? Where did she come from, and where did she go for deceiving Merlin with a fate worse than death?

The mists lay heavy over the waters that morning, soft and silver as a dream half-remembered. On the far shore, Queen Elaine of Benoic fled the smoking ruins of her castle, her son clutched to her breast. Behind her, the banners of her enemies fluttered like black wings, and the air carried the sound of a dying kingdom. She stumbled to the edge of a still, deep lake, its surface so smooth it seemed a mirror to another world. The boy in her arms—fair-haired, wide-eyed—did not cry. He simply looked toward the water as though something unseen called to him from beneath its glassy skin.

Elaine fell to her knees and raised her voice to the heavens. "God of mercy, save my son from the sword! Take him, if you must, but let him live!" And as her tears fell into the water, the lake began to stir. The ripples spread, widening like the rings of destiny, and from the mist rose a woman of radiant beauty. Her gown shimmered like moonlight on moving water, her hair dark as the deep, and her eyes held the stillness of eternity. Elaine gasped. "Who are you, spirit of the lake?" The woman smiled, though there was sadness in it. "I am she whom men shall call *the Lady of the Lake*. Fear not, queen of Benoic. The child you hold is chosen. His path is written among the stars."

"Chosen?" Elaine whispered. "For what?" "For greatness—and for sorrow," the Lady replied. "He will be the purest of knights, the bravest of hearts. Yet love will test him, and through that love, kingdoms shall tremble." The queen looked down at her son. The boy's small hand reached out toward the shining woman as though he already knew her. "Give him to me," said the Lady softly. "For here, beneath the waters, I shall raise him safe from the evils of men. He shall learn honour, compassion, and strength. And when the time is right, he shall return to serve the once and future king." Elaine hesitated—but the fires of war burned behind her, and her heart knew the truth of destiny's call. With one last kiss, she placed the child into the Lady's waiting arms. The enchantress turned and walked upon the water as though it were earth, and as she reached the lake's heart, she and the child sank gently beneath the surface. The ripples closed, and only mist remained.

In the years that followed, beneath the lake's enchanted veil, the boy grew into a youth of noble grace. The Lady of the Lake taught him the language of the stars, the songs of the sword, and the sacred code of knighthood. She guided his hand in battle craft and tempered his spirit with wisdom.

She loved him as one might love a son—but her love was tinged with the calm distance of the divine, for she knew that he was not hers to keep.

When at last the time came, she summoned him to the water's edge. The mists parted to reveal a gleaming world above, bright with dawn. In her hands, she held a sword of exquisite beauty, its blade alive with light. "Lancelot," she said, naming him for the first time, "you are ready. Go forth into the world of men. Seek out King Arthur and serve him well. Let your sword defend the weak, let your honour shine above all, and let your heart love truly—though that love may yet undo you."

He knelt before her, his head bowed. "My lady, you have been my mother, my guide, and my soul. How shall I live without your light?" She touched his brow with gentle fingers. "You will find my light wherever truth and love endure. Go now, my knight of the lake." And so he rose from the waters like a vision reborn, stepping onto the mortal shore. The sunlight caught his armour.

From that day on, the world would know him as Sir Lancelot du Lac—Lancelot of the Lake—warrior, lover, and legend. Far behind him, in the deep, still waters, the Lady watched quietly. A single tear slipped from her cheek, rippling outward until it vanished in the depths. She knew, as all immortals do, that even the purest heart cannot escape the wheel of fate turning.

Well, we now know the fate of Lancelot and the enchantment of Nyneve, the lady of the Lake, upon Merlin. She suffered much for the death of her adopted son and for the tricks she played upon Merlin to extract his secrets from him. Into the forest of adventure, Nyneve hurried restlessly. She had changed since, as an impatient and ambitious girl, she had robbed Merlin of his secrets and, some say, his life. Back then, she wanted power and influence without understanding the price that life demands for such gains. But over the years, her power had imprisoned her own heart just as she once entrapped Merlin. Because of her magic, she could do things ordinary folk could not, and rather than setting her free, this made her enslaved to the helpless. Her gift of healing made her well sought after to cure the sick, and her powers tied her to the unfortunate.

Alas, while her strength bound her to the weak and troubled, it did not bind them to him, for they did not offer friendship in payment for their debt. Thus Nyneve found herself alone and lonely, praised but desolate, she longed for the old times when love and kindness were cast equally into a coffer by all, for there is no loneliness like that of one who can only give, and no anger like that of those who only receive and bear the weight of debt. She stayed little in any one place, for gladness for her services invariably changed to uneasiness in the face of her power.

In her isolation, she recalled the wonderful times she had with Lancelot when he was growing up. It was before she had deceived Merlin, and now she was paying the price. Little did the world know that they, in fact, lived in a cave behind the waterfall at the edge of the lake. Whilst she may have used her inherited sorcery and magic to give the impression she lived in the lake, it was not so.

It was in a recall of Lancelot as a young man that she, whilst travelling in a forest, came upon a young squire weeping. When she quieted in him, he revealed that a lady had betrayed his beloved master; and now the master's heart was broken, and he lay arms wide, awaiting death. Take me to your Lord." Nyeve said. " He shall not die for love of any unworthy woman. If she is merciless in love, the proper punishment is to love and yet be unloved." So the squire escorted her to the bedside of his master, Sir Pellas, who lay with hollow cheeks and fevered brow.

Why does good throw itself under the feet of evil?" she said, and soothed his throbbing head with her cool hand. She sang to him, and her magic brought peace and the enchantment of dreamless sleep. Then she sought out the treacherous lady, who called herself Ettarde, and brought her to the bed of the sleeping Pellas, saying, "How do you dare to bring death to such a man?" Then, for an instant, she recalled what she had done to Merlin and was full of remorse. "What are you that you could not bring kindness?" I offer you now the pain you have inflicted on another. Already, you feel my spell and are beginning to love this man. You love him more than anything in the world. You would die for him, so deeply do you love him." For Ettarde caught the spell and repeated: "I love him. " Oh God, I love him. How can I love what I earlier despised?" Nyneve whispered in her ear: "It's a little parcel of hell you won't offer others." Then Nyneve whispered in the sleeping knight's ear, awakening him, stepping back to watch. When Pelles caught sight of Ettarde, he was filled with loathing for her, and, when her loving hand moved towards him, he shrank back in disgust.' Go away. "He cried, " I cannot stand the sight of you, for you are treacherous and cold." leave me and never let me see you again." Ettarde fell to the ground, weeping. " Nyneve said: " Now you know the pain. Now you know what he felt for you."

"I love him", Ettarde screamed. "You will always love him. And you will die with your love unwanted; and that is a dry, shivering death. Go now to your dusty death," commanded Nyneve. Then Nyneve returned to Pellas and said. "Rise, Sir Knight, and begin to live again. One day you will find true love, and she will find you." Pelles responde " I am over it all." Nyneve responded, " Not so. I promise to stay until you find your love." And so it was that they lived happily ever after.

Percival, the Late Knight.

The dawn broke pale over the western hills, its first light striking the weathered towers of Camelot. Within the echoing hall, the Knights of the Round Table gathered, their banners tattered from years of war. But one seat—a straightforward chair of polished oak —remained empty. That seat belonged to Sir Percival, the knight who was ever late, yet never absent.

Before he wore armour or carried a sword, Percival had been a wild boy of the woods. His father, once a noble knight, had fallen in battle, and his mother raised him far from the world of men, fearful he might share the same fate. But the blood of knighthood ran strong in him, and from his youth he dreamed of Camelot—the shining city of Arthur, the noble fellowship of the Round Table. He trained himself in secret, wrestling with tree trunks and chasing deer through the glades until he could match their speed.

One spring morning, a party of knights passed through his forest, their armour flashing like stars through the leaves. Percival, awestruck, followed them until the last rider turned and said kindly, "Why, shadow young woodsman?" The boy, his eyes fierce with wonder. "I would be one of you, A knight of the Round Table."
The knights laughed gently, thinking him a dreamer, but one among them—Sir Gawain—saw something in the boy's bearing that stirred respect. "Then come to Camelot," said Gawain. "If you dare to stand before Arthur's throne, perhaps your dream may yet live."

And so Percival's journey began.

His travels were long and perilous. He fought brigands, crossed frozen passes, and wandered through lands broken by war. In a lonely valley, he came upon a knight clad in black, a sworn enemy of Arthur's realm. The stranger mocked him: "You, a knight? You wear no spurs, bear no crest, and know not the code of chivalry."

"I fight for honour," Percival said simply, drawing his blade.
The duel was fierce and swift. Though untested, Percival's courage burned hotter than his fear. In the end, he struck the foe down and took from him a fine sword—a weapon forged by a smith of Avalon, its hilt bound in silver. He carried it back to Camelot, a token of victory for his king.

But fate would not let him rest. For on the road home, he encountered another knight—this one bearing Arthur's crest. But the man's words were filled with venom; he plotted secretly against the king and the fellowship of the Round Table.

Percival's heart turned cold. "You wear the Lion of Camelot, yet speak with the tongue of a serpent." The man reached for his sword, but Percival was quicker. With a cry to heaven, he struck down the traitor and cast his broken crest into the dust.

When he reached Camelot at last, he knelt before Arthur and laid the two swords at his feet. "My liege," he said, "I have slain both your enemy and your betrayer. Grant me leave to serve you in honour, that I may right what others wrong."

Arthur looked upon him with wonder. "Rise, Sir Percival," he said. "You have fought not for glory, but for truth. Such men I count among the noblest of knights."

And so Percival's seat at the Round Table was filled.

Years went by, and Camelot faded under Mordred's treachery. When the call to arms sounded, Percival was far from the court, guarding pilgrims along the dangerous northern roads. He rode tirelessly to reach the battlefield, but the fight was already underway—the air heavy with dust and shouts. He charged through the smoke like a thunderbolt, his sword ringing out, his banner torn. Three times he broke the enemy lines; three times he lifted fallen mates from the blood-soaked ground.

When Arthur fell beneath Mordred's spear, it was Percival who carried him from the field and wept over his broken body. The dream of Camelot had ended—but Percival's loyalty had not.
In time, when the surviving knights returned to the ruined hall, Percival came too late as ever. The torches burned low, and silence hung like a veil.

He bowed his head before the remaining fellowship. "Forgive me, brothers. I have been late to the call. Yet my heart has never wavered."

Sir Gawain, old and wounded, smiled faintly. "Nay, Percival. A knight who comes late but true is worth more than one who comes early in deceit." They raised their cups in honour of Arthur, of the fallen, and of the dream they had built. And when the dawn broke over Camelot's crumbling towers, the light touched Percival's helm as though the sun itself remembered his faith. He was the last to leave the hall—silent, steadfast, and alone. But those who came after would tell his story as that of the knight who never abandoned the dream, though he was always the last to arrive.

The smoke of battle had long faded, and Camelot stood silent.
Its towers, once bright as morning, now lay broken beneath ivy and shadow. The Round Table was empty, its circle unbroken only in

memory. And in the vast stillness of that fallen dream, one knight yet lingered — Sir Percival, the last who had fought for Arthur and lived. He wandered the empty hall where dust and silence spoke more truth than any words. Upon the king's throne lay the crown, tarnished and forgotten, its gold dimmed by the breath of time. Percival knelt before it and whispered, "My liege, your kingdom is no more. Yet your vision lives within me. I shall guard it, though the world forgets." He rose, took his sword and shield, and set out alone. For many nights, he rode through the wilderness, guided only by the stars. He passed villages laid waste, forests burned by war, and rivers red with memory. But in his dreams, he began to hear a voice — soft, sorrowful, and holy."Seek me, Percival. Seek the Cup of the Christ. Seek the Grail that was once held above Arthur's head, when he took his first communion, and the chalice rose like light itself."

He awoke each dawn with tears upon his cheeks, for he knew the voice was not of this world. It was the echo of Merlin's prophecy, the whisper of faith that had bound Arthur's kingdom to Heaven. And so, Percival set his course toward the west, to the lands beyond the sea where legend said Avalon slept.

Then, whilst venturing through a forest, he hears the voice of his dream again, " The road you trod is never free of trail. Three times you will be tested. The first, by Hunger, the second by Pride and the third by Desire." Then the voice was silent.

So, whilst trudging through a barren vale after being without food or drink for days, he came across a beautiful maiden who offered him food. He impulsively eats her food without thinking of the consequences that may follow as a result of this innocent act.

During his travels, Percival reaches the Fisher King's castle. He witnesses a procession featuring a mysterious bleeding lance and the Holy Grail. He had been warned not to ask too many questions, but his adherence to this advice is taken to an extreme. In his own pride, he remains silent, failing to ask the meaning of the procession, and he fails to heal the wounded king and the Wasteland. This failure is a test of his perception and a consequence of following empty protocol rather than seeking true meaning.

Then, in his quest, he comes upon the beautiful maiden again, who this time offers him wine to drink. But no sooner had he put the cup to his lips than he found that it was not full of wine but of blood. Then, looking down at the hilt of his sword, which reminded him of his knightly vows and his religious duty, he raised his sword, thinking the maiden was a witch who was attempting to seduce him. He makes the sign of the cross, and the demon disappears in a cloud of smoke. As penance for his near-fall, Percival wounds himself. This final act of resistance and repentance is the ultimate test that proves his worthiness to achieve the Grail. So then he hears the voice of his dreams once more.

" There is no Grail, no God, no hope. Camelot is dust."

And with that, the illusion vanished like mist.

And so, having triumphed not by sword but by spirit, Percival passed beyond temptation into grace. When dawn came, he found himself standing beside a still lake, and there, above the mist, appeared Halo, the angel of glassblowers, who fashioned a crystal chalice that hovered over the water, rising as the Holy Grail — radiant, alive, and unearthly.

Percival touched the chalice, and it turned into the clay vessel, the Grail, which Christ used to share bread and wine with his Apostles at the Last Supper, which every good Friar had reenacted since time immemorial to do this in commemoration of Christ. Percival wrapped the Grail in his cloak & rode off to Camelot to give it to King Arthur, who helped keep the secret of where it was to be concealed again with the Ark of the Covenant. Precival then knelt with tears on his cheeks and whispered, "Now I see, my Lord — the quest was never to find, but to become."

Far away, deep within the ancient forest of Broceliande, Merlin watched. Though long unseen by mortal eyes, the old enchanter still walked the earth — not in flesh, but as a spirit of wind and memory, bound between worlds. He had foreseen all that had come to pass: the fall of Arthur, the ruin of Camelot, the scattering of the Knights. Yet even in prophecy, one truth had escaped him — that from the wreckage of pride would rise the quiet light of grace. Through the veil of time, he beheld Percival kneeling beside the still lake, the Grail's light reflected in his tear-streaked face. Merlin bowed his head, and for the first time in an age, he smiled.

When the sun rose over the broken towers of Camelot, the air hung heavy with silence. Sir Percival, pale with weariness but radiant with purpose, rode slowly through the ruined gates. Across his saddle, wrapped in his cloak of faded crimson, he bore the Holy Grail — its light dimmed now to a soft, inner glow, as though it slept, dreaming of the hearts it had tested and redeemed. The surviving knights gathered in awe as Percival entered the great hall. Where once laughter and music had filled the air, now only the wind whispered through shattered windows.

With reverence, Percival laid the Grail before King Arthur.
The King's face, lined with sorrow and wisdom, softened as he beheld it. He lifted the sacred vessel in both hands, and for a moment, the hall was filled with golden light. No one spoke. Even the torches seemed to bow their flames.

Arthur turned to his knights and said, "The Grail has returned to us, not through conquest, but through purity. Yet this light must not remain in the hands of men, for greed and pride will seek it again. I shall carry it to a place beyond corruption — where it shall rest beside the Ark of the Covenant, and together they shall be kept until the hearts of men are worthy once more." A murmur rose among the knights, part awe, part grief. They knew the King was taking the first steps of his final journey.

When Arthur departed with the Grail, the remaining knights sat wearily around the broken Round Table. Their armour was tarnished, their eyes hollow with remorse. The Table, once a perfect circle of unity, now bore a great crack through its centre — as if heaven itself had struck it with lightning. They saw in it a mirror of themselves: brave, loyal, but broken. They had expelled Mordred and the deceiving knights who had plotted for the throne, seeking to claim Camelot's glory for their own. And among those cast out was Lancelot, though not as an enemy, for he had made peace with Arthur, pledging to forsake his forbidden love for Queen Guinevere and to live henceforth in honour and repentance.

Arthur's mercy had bound them once more in friendship, yet he wound in their fellowship still bled unseen. Each knight, in his heart, felt the weight of destiny pressing close — the sense that the final reckoning was drawing near. The air itself seemed to darken; the earth waited in silence.

They sat there — the last of the true knights of Camelot — weary, watchful, and remorseful, awaiting the King's return. For word had come that Mordred, in exile, was gathering the lost, the bitter, and the faithless beneath his blackened banner. And soon, Arthur would return — not to rule in peace, but to ride to war. A battle not merely of men, but of faith against despair…Father against son, light against darkness, the crown against the shadow.

In Arthur's camp, in the night before the final battle, the Grail's light still lingered within him, faint as a candle beneath the storm.

He prayed not for victory, but for mercy — that the souls of those who fell, friend and foe alike, might find peace. When he rose, his armour gleamed not with polish, but with quiet purpose, as though the Grail itself had blessed him for what must come.

Not far from him stood Sir Lancelot, his face shadowed with remorse. The years of guilt had weighed heavily upon him, yet tonight his spirit was evident. The King had forgiven him he had once betrayed, and now he sought only one thing — to die in Arthur's service, and through that death, to redeem his life.

He looked to the east, where the clouds glowed faintly red, and whispered, "For love I sinned; for love I shall atone." Around them, the remaining knights of the Round Table knelt in a circle.

Their armour was dented, their banners torn, but in their eyes burned the old fire of brotherhood. They were the remnants of a dream — the last guardians of an age soon to pass. Each carried within him a single prayer: that this final battle might save what was left of Camelot's soul.

Some prayed for peace, others for courage, and a few for forgiveness. Yet all knew the same truth: that dawn would bring the reckoning foretold by Merlin long ago —the clash of father and son, of light and shadow, of heaven's will and man's despair.

The Last Battle.

In the King's tent, Arthur knelt beside his sword Excalibur, its edge resting upon the earth. He bowed his head and murmured, "O Lord of Hosts, give me strength — not to conquer, but to endure." Outside, thunder rolled across the hills. And so the last night of Camelot passed — not in glory, but in prayer.

In that twilight, Melin saw the vision he had long feared —
The Round Table broken, Camelot aflame, and Arthur struck down by the son he never knew he had. The prophecy was complete. The dream he had sown in men's hearts would wither before morning. "So it comes to pass," he murmured, his voice no stronger than the sigh of the tide. "All that is built upon the heart of man must fall to dust. Yet from that dust, perhaps, a greater truth may rise."
His heart trembled with sorrow — not for himself, but for Arthur, the boy he had once guided, the king he had loved as a son.
He remembered the day he had placed the sword in the stone, the moment when destiny had chosen its bearer. Now, he could only watch as that destiny turned upon itself.

He sought to call the spirits of air and fire, but his words faltered.
His magic — once as swift and sure as breath — had grown dim.
The elements no longer obeyed him; the earth no longer stirred at his command. Even the voice of Nineve, the Lady of the Lake, came to him faint and distant, as though she were already part of another world. "Merlin," she whispered upon the wind, "Your time among men is ending. The pattern you wove has run its course. The child of your dream must walk alone now."

He lowered his head, the weight of centuries upon him. "Then let it be so," he said. "I have seen what must be, and I accept it. For even the greatest enchantment cannot bind eternity." And as he turned away, the world around him began to fade — not in darkness, but in light. The stones shimmered like glass, the air grew still, and the great enchanter felt himself drawn into the hidden realm beneath the hill — where time sleeps and dreams are kept for the world to remember. Thus Merlin passed from mortal sight, neither dead nor truly gone, but waiting — as all prophecy waits — for the hour when Britain's need is greatest.

Dawn came grey and hollow over the plain of Camlann.

The wind carried the scent of iron and rain, and the ravens wheeled above as if they already knew the outcome.

Across the valley, two armies faced one another — Arthur's loyal knights, weary and thinned by years of strife, and Mordred's host, fierce and desperate, swollen with those who sought power in the ruin of Camelot. Among Arthur's men rode Sir Lancelot, his armour dulled by penance, his heart heavy with regret. He had returned from exile, answering the King's summons not for glory, but for redemption.

Beside him knelt Sir Percival, having kept vigil through the night in prayer and silence. His sword lay before him, the steel kissed by the morning dew, as he whispered a final benediction: "Lord of Light, grant us courage, that the realm may be made whole again." The Round Table was broken, but its spirit yet lived in those few who gathered in readiness to do battle.

Across the valley, Mordred's host gathered like a dark tide — men without faith, knights without honour, wielding the sigils of rebellion. King Arthur, clad in the armour of his youth, rode before his weary men. The sword Excalibur hung at his side — the blade that had been forged in the heart of Avalon, gleaming faintly as though it mourned what was to come.

He looked upon his companions — Lancelot, silent and grim, his face shadowed by guilt; Percival, kneeling in prayer beside his horse; and the few who still bore the emblem of the Round Table upon their shields.

At first, Arthur considered entrusting Excalibur to Lancelot in case he fell in battle. His final wish was that, should he die, Excalibur be returned to the Lady of the Lake, Lancelot's adopted mother. It would be too much for his brotherly knight, so he turned to some-one else.

Among those, Sir Bedivere, one of the nobles of the Knights of the Round Table, whose only fault was being hesitant to act on matters of importance, it was to him that King Arthur entrusted his Excal-ibur sword in the event of being killed in battle. "My King, my brother," Bedivere whispered. Arthur smiled faintly, his voice no louder than a sigh. Arthur turned to Lancelot: "You are forgiven, old friend. I give Excalibur to Bedivere to return it to the lake. There lies Britain's hope." Lancelot understood and acknowledged Arthur's choice.

The sky darkened with storm and smoke. Lightning split the clouds as if heaven itself could not bear witness to what was unfolding below. Steel clashed upon steel, and the field of Camlann was soaked in the blood of friend and foe alike. Cries of valour, pain, and fury echoed through the valley, mingling with the screams of dying horses and the clash of broken shields.
King Arthur rode at the head of his host, his armour battered, his banner torn. Excalibur, gleaming like captured sunlight, rose and fell with deadly grace. Around him, the few loyal knights of the Round Table fought with desperate courage — Lancelot, grim and silent; Percival, praying as he struck; and the remnants of Camelot's once-noble company, standing their ground against the darkness.

The climax came when Mordred faced Arthur. Launching his spear, he fatally wounded Arthur, who collapsed to the ground in his final breath. Mordred charged forward, sword raised, to deliver the killing blow. However, the ever-vigilant Lancelot countered with a strike like a lightning bolt, and the deceiver fell dying beside Arthur.

"Father" Mordred whispered, his voice fading like a distant echo, "I see now… the light you sought." Arthur, barely breathing, reached up and stroked his son's hair. A single tear slid down Mordred's cheek. "You are forgiven, my son," he murmured. "In love, we are made whole." And so they lay — father and son — their hands joined, the battle fading into the background. The storm raged above, rain falling like heaven's own lament, washing away the blood of kings. As their last breath escaped, a strange calm settled over the field. Those still alive swore they saw two lights rise together from the fallen — twin flames ascending into the clouds —and the mists of Avalon rolled in to claim them both.

When the last of the thunder faded, the field of Camlann lay still. No sound broke the silence save for the sigh of the wind through torn banners and the distant cries of ravens circling above the dead. The dream of Camelot, born of faith and bound by honour, had come to its end in blood and rain. Through the smoke, Sir Lancelot, his armour darkened and his heart broken. He dismounted and knelt beside the fallen King, cradling Arthur's head upon his lap. The once-mighty hand that had drawn Excalibur from the stone now hung limp, its strength spent.

The rain washed their faces, mingling tears with the water of the heavens. Then came a soft light — faint but pure — rising from Arthur's breast. The King's eyes opened once more, and he spoke, though his voice was little more than a breath: "Take me to the water. Excalibur must return to the hand from which it came. Only then shall the circle be complete."

Lancelot nodded, and together he and Percival carried Arthur to the shores of a quiet lake beyond the battlefield — its surface calm, unbroken, untouched by war.

There, Arthur spoke his final words.

"The sword was never mine. It belonged to the spirit of the land. Hand it to Belvidere, my friend, and let the Lady of the Lake keep it until Britain requires me again."

As formally instructed, he handed Excalibur to Sir Belvidere. Lancelot and the knights of the Round Table, now once more united, carried Arthur's body to the water's edge and peered down at the dead king's illuminated face. He appears to be just sleeping, although they know his spirit had left the body. They set him upon a barge and headed it afloat towards the mystical Island of Avalon.

Then, as the story went, Sir Belvidere, on his king's orders, rode to the lake with the intention of throwing Excelibut into the depths. Sometimes he hesitated before gathering the will and strength to throw the sword into the water from which it had come, into the still waters where the mists of Avalon gathered.

As he threw it in, a pale arm — the Lady of the Lake's — rose from the water, caught the blade by its hilt, and pulled it beneath the surface. The water rippled to the shore, and like all things in life, they faded away, leaving the lake silent once more. When he returned to meet his fellow knights, Arthur was gone. Only Percival was there, gazing towards the western horizon where a barge shrouded in silver mist drifted away — And upon it lay the once and future king, taken to Avalon, where he would sleep until the world called for him again.

And Merlin, in the shadow of a dream, remembered the day he had placed the sword in the stone, the moment when destiny had chosen its bearer. Now, he could only watch as that destiny turned upon itself. He sought to call the spirits of air and fire, but his words faltered. His magic — once as swift and sure as breath — had grown dim. The elements no longer obeyed him; the earth no longer stirred at his command. Even the voice of the Lady of the Lake came to him faint and distant, as though she were already part of another world. "Merlin," she whispered upon the wind.

The wind swept cold across the high ridges of the Pyrenees, carrying with it the scent of pine, earth, and memory. A solitary pilgrim climbed the stony path, his cloak weathered, his staff worn smooth from many miles. His hair was white as frost, his beard long and silvered by the years, yet his eyes — deep and ageless — held the light of another time. For this was Merlin, the once-great enchanter, now a wanderer in the age of faith.

He paused upon a crag above Roncesvalles Pass, gazing down into the green valley below — the place where, long ago, the mighty Roland, paladin of France, had fought his last battle. Merlin bowed his head. He could almost hear the echo of Roland's horn, Olifant, calling across the centuries — the cry of courage and sacrifice that never fades. "Here, too," he murmured, "a hero fell defending his faith... and his story became legend."

He remembered Rustichello da Pisa, the poet who had once journeyed this same way in the twelfth century — a chronicler of kings, who, like a dreamer guided by unseen hand, had penned anew the tale of Arthur and his knights. It was through him that the myth of Camelot was reborn — and Merlin smiled faintly, knowing whose whisper had stirred the poet's mind.

He looked westward.

The clouds drifted low, touched with gold by the setting sun.
Far beyond the mountains lay Santiago de Compostel**a**, the end of the pilgrim road — the resting place of Saint James, Apostle of Christ, whose bones, it was said, slept beneath the great altar.

Merlin pressed on. He passed shepherds and fellow travellers who thought he was a quiet old bloke heading off to pray. But in truth, he kept to himself not for penance, but to remember. He thought of Arthur, the boy who had pulled the sword from the stone. Of Lancelot, whose heart was torn between love and loyalty.
Of Percival, the pure knight who found the Grail. Of the Lady of the Lake, who had once held him in her gaze like a spell, and whose memory still haunted him as softly as the breeze through the trees.

When he reached the plain beyond Navarra, the towers of Santiago flickered faintly on the horizon — their spires towering like prayers carved in stone. He felt the pull of destiny once more.

"So many swords drawn," he whispered. "So many kings fallen… yet the truest victory is not of steel, but of the soul."

In the quiet of the evening, he entered the Cathedral of Santiago. Pilgrims knelt in prayer, the air thick with incense and the golden light of candles. Before the high altar stood the image of Saint James, the Apostle of the Grail, whose cup symbolised the body and blood of Christ — the very mystery Arthur had sought to understand.

Merlin fell to his knees. He closed his eyes, and for a moment he was no longer old — he was the voice of ages, the keeper of dreams. He saw again the sacred chamber hidden deep beneath the earth, where the Holy Grail rested beside the Ark of the Covenant, untouched by time, guarded by silence. And Merlin sighed, and his heart fluted in remembrance, for in him the spirit of all those who once lived in his dreams was gone, but there in was Camelot, and to him it would never die.

When dawn broke, the pilgrims got up and kept on their way. But the old bloke was gone. Only his staff was left, leaning against the stone, with faint letters carved into it, saying:

"The once and future King shall rise again — when the world is ready to believe."

So Merlin once again became part of legend, his journey ending not in magic, but in faith. And it is told that Merlin, the wanderer, walked the pilgrim road long before it was worn smooth by the feet of men. In every age, his spirit has returned — not in robe or crown, but in the quiet hearts of those who search for truth upon the open road.

They say that when the wind sweeps down from the Pyrenees and touches the pilgrims' faces with cool breath, it is Merlin passing by — unseen, yet felt — reminding them that all quests begin and end within. And Merlin waits not in castle nor tower, but in the heart of every pilgrim who dares to dream of a better world — a world where courage is tempered by mercy, and where the light of the Grail still shines in the hands of those who believe.

And so, as the pilgrim walks onward to Santiago, each footstep echoes with the whisper of ancient promise: *"The King shall return... when the world is once more worthy of his dream."*

Silence reigned in Compostela as pilgrims knelt, awaiting the celebration of their completed mission. Then a friar ascended the pulpit, his voice rising above the choir.

You who have walked the Way — you have journeyed through time itself. You have treaded the paths of kings and saints, poets and dreamers. You have remembered the myths of the ages — of Arthur, Roland, and the pilgrims of old — those who moved from darkness into light. But now, my brothers and sisters, it is time to truly live — to live fully. The Way does not end at Santiago. It begins anew in the heart that has been changed. Carry with you not the sword of war, but the light of love. The Grail is not a cup, but a spirit — the divine spark that resides within us all.

The cathedral fell into reverent silence. Among the bowed heads, the pilgrim with the silver hair lifted his gaze. A single tear traced the line of his cheek, reflecting the candlelight.

And so it is said that Merlin, the eternal wanderer, walks still.
Not in flesh, but in spirit — beside each pilgrim who takes the road in search of faith and redemption.

The Camino de Santiago isn't just a trail of earth and stone,
but a mirror of the soul — a journey from sword to chalice, from pride to grace. It may well have been the template of Merlin's dream all along.

It is said when the winds come up upon the desert plains of Najrera on The Camino Way to Santiago, some hear a whisper — a voice old as the world: *"The dream of Camelot is not lost. It sleeps within you."*

And somewhere, beyond the veil of time, the Round Table gleams once more. Arthur sits among his knights, Lancelot at his side, Percival guarding the Grail. And watching, ever patient, stands Merlin — the pilgrim who never ceased to believe.

"The King shall return," the wind murmurs, *"when the hearts of men are worthy of his dream."* Merlin once more repeated.

And for this old author, a modern-day scribe for Merlin's legends and the swords he encountered, he left the enclosure of the Cathedral— Outside, the sun broke over the spires, and the bells of Santiago rang out across the land—calling not to battle, but to peace. There, pilgrims lifted their faces to the light, their burdens falling away like shadows at dawn.

And the old man smiled, for he knew the truth at last: the Grail had never been lost — it had simply waited for hearts made humble by the journey to find it again.

And as he passed into the light, no one saw the faint shimmer of gold that trailed behind him, the last glimmer of Merlin's magic, woven forever into the Way of the Pilgrims, into the stones of the road, the whisper of the wind, and the hearts of all who still seek the light beyond the mist. For the dream of Camelot does not die —it only waits to be remembered, each time a soul sets forth upon the path, carrying within the sword of courage, the dream of fulfilment, and the glory of what once was, be it myth or reality.

About the Author:

Doug McPhillips, poet, singer, songwriter, and author, commenced his journey of discovery over a decade ago after life-changing experiences.

The many tracks he has travelled through the Northern Hemisphere and down under in Australia and New Zealand have contributed to the facts, fictions, and beliefs about the novel's spiritual essence.

Doug has authored twenty-five books, many of which focus on personal spiritual growth and belief. He has also produced and recorded three albums of songs inspired by his travels and experiences.

Doug is an adventurer who divides his time between family and friends, his creative pursuits, and those who benefit most from his efforts and experience.